'It's good to see you up.' Stefano hooked an arm around Anna's waist, dropped a kiss on the nape of her neck and inhaled her delicious soft floral scent.

Turning his back on her in the early hours of the night had been hard, but necessary. He'd sensed her desire simmering beneath her rigid surface and known that with only a little persuasion on his part she would be his for the taking. But it was too soon. When he seduced her anew he wanted his wife to be a tinderbox of desire for him. He wanted her to beg for his possession. He wanted her helpless to do anything but melt in his arms. He wanted her fully fit and knowing exactly what she was doing.

The more heightened her emotions and her desire for him, the greater the low that would follow when he exacted his revenge.

Michelle Smart's love affair with books started when she was a baby, when she would cuddle them in her cot. A voracious reader of all genres, she found her love of romance established when she stumbled across her first Mills & Boon book at the age of twelve. She's been reading—and writing them—ever since. Michelle lives in Northamptonshire with her husband, and two young Smarties.

Books by Michelle Smart

Mills & Boon Modern Romance

The Perfect Cazorla Wife
The Russian's Ultimatum
The Rings that Bind

Brides for Billionaires

Married for the Greek's Convenience

One Night With Consequences

Claiming His Christmas Consequence

Wedlocked!

Wedded, Bedded, Betrayed

The Kalliakis Crown

Talos Claims His Virgin
Theseus Discovers His Heir
Helios Crowns His Mistress

The Irresistible Sicilians

What a Sicilian Husband Wants
The Sicilian's Unexpected Duty
Taming the Notorious Sicilian

Visit the Author Profile page at millsandboon.co.uk for more titles.

ONCE A
MORETTI WIFE

BY
MICHELLE SMART

MILLS &
BOON

First Published in Great Britain 2017
By Mills & Boon, an imprint of HarperCollins*Publishers*
1 London Bridge Street, London, SE1 9GF

© 2017 Michelle Smart

ISBN: 978-0-263-06865-8

Our policy is to use papers that are natural, renewable and recyclable
products and made from wood grown in sustainable forests. The logging
and manufacturing processes conform to the legal environmental
regulations of the country of origin.

Printed and bound in Great Britain
by CPI Antony Rowe, Chippenham, Wiltshire

ONCE A
MORETTI WIFE

This book is for Jennifer Hayward,
writer extraordinaire and a wonderful friend. xxx

CHAPTER ONE

How much had she *drunk*?

Anna Robson clutched her head, which pounded as if the force of a hundred hammers were battering it.

There was a lump there. She prodded it cautiously and winced. Had she hit her head?

She racked her aching, confused brain, trying hard to remember. She'd gone out for a drink with Melissa, hadn't she? *Hadn't* she?

Yes. She had. She'd gone for a drink with her sister after their Spinning class, as they did every Thursday evening.

She peered at her bedside clock and gave a start—her phone's alarm should have gone off an hour ago. Where had she put it?

Still holding her head, she looked around but saw no sight of it, then forgot all about it as her stomach rebelled. She only just made it to the bathroom in time to vomit.

Done, she sat loose-limbed like a puppet on the floor, desperately trying to remember what she'd drunk. She wasn't a heavy drinker at the best of times and on a work night she would stick to a small glass of white wine. But right then, she felt as if she'd drunk a dozen bottles.

There was no way she could go into the office... But

then she remembered she and Stefano had a meeting with a young tech company he was interested in buying. Stefano had tasked Anna, as he always did, with going through the company's accounts, reports and claims and producing her own summary. He trusted her judgement. If it concurred with his then he would invest in the company. If her judgement differed he would rethink his strategy. Stefano wanted her report first thing so he could digest it before the meeting.

She'd have to email it and beg illness.

But, after staggering cautiously around the flat she shared with Melissa, holding onto the walls for support, she realised she must have left her laptop at the office. She'd have to phone Stefano. He could open it himself. She'd give him the password, although she was ninety-nine per cent certain he'd hacked it at least once already.

All she had to do was find her phone. Walking carefully to the kitchen, she found a pretty handbag on the counter. Next to it was an envelope addressed with her name.

She blinked hard to keep her eyes focused and pulled the letter out. She attempted to read it a couple of times but none of it made any sense. It was from Melissa asking for Anna's forgiveness for her trip to Australia and promising to call when she got there.

Australia? Melissa must be having a joke at her expense, although her sister saying she was going to visit the mother who'd abandoned them a decade ago wasn't the slightest bit funny to Anna's mind. The letter's postscript did explain one thing though—Melissa said she'd gritted the outside step of the front door so Anna wouldn't slip on it again, and asked her to see a doctor if her head hurt where she'd banged it.

Anna put her hand to the lump on the side of her head. She had no recollection whatsoever of slipping. And no recollection of any ice. The early November weather had been mild but now, as she looked through the kitchen window, she saw a thick layer of frost.

Her head hurting too much for her to make sense of anything, she put the letter to one side and had a look in the handbag. The purse she'd used for a decade, threadbare but clinging to life, was in it. It had been the last gift from her father before he'd died. Had she swapped handbags with Melissa? That wouldn't be unusual; Anna and Melissa were always lending each other things. What *was* unusual was that Anna didn't remember. But they must have swapped because in the bottom of the pretty bag also sat Anna's phone. That was another mystery solved.

She pulled it out and saw she had five missed calls. Struggling to focus, she tapped in the pin code to unlock it.

Wrong pin. She tried again. *Wrong pin.*

Sighing, she shoved it back in the bag. It took enough effort to stay on her feet, never mind remembering a code with a head that felt like fog. It was times like this that she cursed their decision to disconnect the landline.

Fine. She'd flag a cab and go to the office, explain that she was dying and then come home again.

Before getting dressed, she took some headache tablets and prayed her tender belly could keep them down.

She always put the next day's clothes on her bedroom chair and now she hugged them to her chest and gingerly sat back on her bed. Where had *this* dress come from? Melissa must have muddled their clothes up again. Not having the energy to hunt for something else, Anna decided to wear it. It was a black long-sleeved, knee-length jersey dress with a nice amount of swish at the hem but it took her an age to get it on, her limbs feeling as if they'd had lead injected into them.

Damn, her *head*.

She didn't have the energy to put on any make-up either, so she made do with running a brush gently through her hair and then she staggered to the front door.

On the rack in the entrance porch was a pair of funky black boots with thick soles she hadn't seen before. Surely Melissa wouldn't mind her borrowing them. That was the best thing about living with her sister; they were the same dress and shoe size.

She locked the front door and treaded carefully down the steps. Finally luck was on her side—a vacant black cab drove up her street within a minute.

She got the driver to drop her off across the road from the futuristic skyscraper near Tower Bridge from where Stefano ran his European operations. As Anna waited at the pedestrian crossing next to the road heaving with traffic, a shiny stretched black Mercedes pulled up outside the front of the building. A doorman opened the back door, and out came Stefano.

The green light flashed and, working on autopilot, she crossed the road, her eyes focused on Stefano rather than where she was walking.

A tall blonde woman got out of the car behind him. Anna didn't recognise her but there was something familiar about her face that made it feel as if nails clawed into Anna's already tender stomach.

A briefcase whacked her in the back and, startled, Anna realised she'd come to a stop in the middle of the road, dozens of other pedestrians jostling around her, some swearing.

Clutching a hand to her stomach to stem the surging rise of nausea, she forced her leaden legs to work and managed to make it to the pavement without being knocked over.

She went through the revolving doors of the building itself, put her bag on the scanner, waited for it to be cleared, then went straight to the bathroom, into the first empty cubicle, and vomited.

Cold perspiration breaking out all over, she knew she was an idiot to have come in. Her hangover—was it a hangover? She'd never felt anything like this—was, if that was possible, getting worse.

Out of the cubicle, after she'd washed her hands and swirled cold water in her mouth, she caught sight of her reflection in the mirror.

She looked awful. Her face was white as a sheet, her dark hair lank around her shoulders...

She did a double take. Had her *hair* grown?

After popping a mint in her mouth, she inched her way around the walls to the elevator. Two men and a woman she vaguely recognised were getting into it, chatting amiably. She slid in with them before the doors closed.

She punched the button for the thirtieth floor and held onto the railing as it began the smooth ride up.

All talk had stopped. She could feel their eyes on her. Did she really look so bad that she'd become a conversation stopper? It was a relief when they got out on the floor below her.

A gaggle of secretaries and administrators worked in the open space in front of the office Anna shared with Stefano. They all turned their heads to stare at her. A couple were open-mouthed.

Did they have to make it so obvious that she looked

this awful? All the same, she managed to get her mouth working enough to smile a greeting. Not one of them responded.

She looked around for Chloe, her newly appointed fresh-faced PA who cowered in terror every time Stefano made an appearance. Poor Chloe would not be happy to know she'd have to take on Anna's duties for the day.

Anna hadn't wanted a PA of her own. *She* was a PA! But Stefano had thrown so many responsibilities her way in the year and a half since he'd poached her from Levon Brothers that when he'd caught her working at nine in the evening, he'd put his foot down and insisted on hiring someone for her.

'Do I get a new job title?' she'd cheekily asked, and been rewarded with a promotion to Executive PA and a hefty pay rise.

Maybe Chloe was cowering in the stationery cupboard, waiting for her arrival so she could hide behind her. The girl would get used to Stefano soon enough. Anna had seen it with most other employees. It was that mixture of awe and fear he inspired that curdled the stomach, but eventually the curdling settled and one could hold a coherent conversation with him.

Anna had skipped all these stages herself but had seen the effect Stefano had on others too many times not to sympathise with it. He inspired terror and hero-worship in equal measure.

She let the office door shut behind her and came to an abrupt halt. For a moment she forgot all about her pounding head and nauseous stomach.

When Stefano had offered her the job and she'd learned it entailed sharing an office with him, she'd said on a whim that she would only do it if he decorated her side in shades of plum. Her memories of her first day working for him were ones of laughter, when she'd walked into the sprawling office and found one half painted a functional cream, the other varying shades of plum.

Today the whole office was cream.

She'd just reached her desk when the door flew open, and Stefano stood there, as dark and menacing as she'd ever seen him.

Before she could ask if he'd had an army of decorators in overnight, he slammed the door shut and folded his arms across his broad chest.

'What are you doing here?'

'Not you too,' she groaned, half in exasperation and half in pain. 'I think I had a fall. I know I look awful but can't you pretend I look like my usual supermodel self?'

It had become one of those long-running jokes between them. Every time Stefano tried to cajole her into coming on a date with him, Anna would make some cutting remark, usually followed by a reminder that his preferred dates were the gorgeous supermodel type, whereas she barely topped five foot.

'You'll get neck-ache if you try to kiss me,' she'd once flippantly told him.

To which he'd immediately replied, *'Shall we find out now?'*

She'd never dared mention kissing to him again. Imagining it was more than enough, and wasn't something she allowed herself to do, not since the one time she'd succumbed to the daydream and then had spent a good week pretending not to have palpitations whenever she got close to him.

There was no denying it, her boss was utterly gorgeous, even when her eyes were struggling to focus as they were now. There was not a single physical aspect of him that didn't make her want to swoon. Well over a foot taller than her, he had hair so dark it looked black, a strong roman nose, generous lips and a chiselled jaw covered in just the right amount of black stubble. He also had eyes capable of arresting a person with one glance; a green colour that could turn from light to dark in a heartbeat. She'd learned to read his eyes well—they corresponded exactly with his mood. Today, they were as dark as they could be.

She wasn't in the right frame of mind to dissect what that meant. The paracetamol she'd taken hadn't made a dent in her headache, which was continuing to get worse by the second. She grabbed the edge of her desk and sat down. Straight away she saw something else that was wrong, even with her double vision. She strained to peer more closely at the clutter on her desk. She never left clutter. It drove her crazy. Everything needed to be in its correct place. And…

'Why are there photos of *cats* on my desk?' She was a dog person, not a cat person. Dogs were loyal. Dogs didn't leave you.

'*Chloe's* desk,' he said in a voice as hard as steel.

Anna tilted her head to look at him and blinked a number of times to focus. Her vision had blurred terribly. 'Don't tease me,' she begged. 'I'm only twenty minutes late. My head feels…'

'I can't believe you would be so brazen to turn up here like this,' he cut in.

Used to Stefano's own brand of English, she assumed his 'brazen' meant 'stupid' or something along those lines. She had to admit, he had a point. Leaving the flat feeling as rotten as she did really did rank as stupid.

'I know I'm not well.' It was an effort to get the words out. 'I feel like death warmed up, but I left my laptop behind and needed to get that report to you. You'll have to get Chloe to sit in on the meeting.'

His jaw clenched and his lips twisted into something that could be either a snarl or a smirk. 'Is this a new tactic?'

Was her hearing now playing up along with the rest of her? One of the things she liked about working for Stefano was that he was a straight talker, regularly taking his more earnest employees to task for their corporate speak. 'I taught myself English,' he would say to them with disdain, 'but if I'd tried learning it from you I would be speaking self-indulgent codswallop.'

She always hid a grin when he said that. 'Self-indulgent codswallop' was a term she'd taught him in her first week working for him. His thick Italian accent made it sound even funnier. She'd taught him a whole heap of insults since; most of which she'd initially directed at him.

Which made his riddle all the more confusing.

'What are you talking about?'

He stepped away from the closed door, nearer to her. 'Have you been taking acting lessons, Mrs Moretti?'

'Mrs...?' She closed her eyes and gave her head a gentle shake, but even that made the hammers trapped in it pound harder. 'Have I woken in the twilight zone?' It didn't sound completely mad when she said it. Quite credible in fact. She'd felt disjointed from the moment she'd woken, Melissa's letter stating that she was flying to Australia only adding to the incoherence.

When she opened her eyes again, she found Stefano by her desk, his large frame swimming before her eyes.

'You're playing an excellent game. Tell me the rules so I know what my next move should be.' His tone was gentle but the menace behind it was unmistakable, his smooth voice decreasing in volume but increasing in danger.

Anna's pretty hazel eyes widened. She had clearly been practising her innocent face in the month since he'd last seen her, Stefano thought scathingly.

It had been a whole month since she'd humiliated him in his own boardroom and walked out of his life.

He placed his hands palm down on her desk and gazed at her, taking in the beautiful face that had captivated him from the start.

'I honestly don't know what you're talking about.' Anna got slowly to her feet. 'I'm going home. One of us is confused about something and I don't know which of us I hope it is.'

He laughed. Oh, she was something else.

'You should go home too,' she said, eying him in much the same manner as a person cornered by a dangerous dog. 'If I didn't know better I'd think you were drunk.'

For a moment he wondered if *she'd* been drinking. Her words had a slurred edge and she seemed unsteady.

But those luscious lips were taunting him. *She* was taunting him, playing a game he hadn't been given the rules to, trying to catch him on the back foot. Well, he wouldn't fall for her games any more. He wrote the rules, not this witch who had spellbound him with lust.

She'd planned it all from the start. She'd deliberately held off his advances for eighteen months so he'd become so desperate to possess her he would agree to marry her just so he could sleep with her.

He'd admit it had been a bit more involved than

that but that had been the crux of it. He'd thought he'd known her. He'd thought he could trust her—*him*, Stefano Moretti, the man who had learned at a young age not to trust anyone.

She'd set him up to marry her so she could divorce him for adultery, humiliating him in front of his staff for good measure, and gain herself a hefty slice of his fortune.

He couldn't believe he'd been stupid enough to fall for it.

When he'd received the call from his lawyer telling him his estranged wife was going to sue him for a fortune, he'd quelled his instinct to race to her home and confront her. He'd forced himself to sit tight.

Sitting tight did not come easily to him. He was not a man to wait for a problem to be solved; he was a man to take a problem by the scruff of the neck and sort it. He reacted. He always had. It was what had got him into so much trouble when he'd been a kid, never knowing when to keep his mouth shut or his fists to himself.

He'd spent nearly two weeks biding his time, refusing to acknowledge her lawyer's letter. In ten days they would have been married for a year and legally able to divorce. Then, and only then, would Anna learn what he was prepared to give her, which was nothing. And he was prepared to make her jump through hoops to reach that knowledge.

He would make her pay for all her lies and deceit. He would only stop when she experienced the equivalent humiliation that he'd been through at her hands.

One hundred million pounds and various assets for barely a year of marriage? Her nerve was beyond incredible.

But despite everything she'd done, seeing her now, his

desire for her remained undiminished. Anna was still the sexiest woman in the world. Classically beautiful, she had shoulder-length silky dark chestnut hair that framed high cheekbones, bee-stung lips that could sting of their own accord and skin as creamy to the touch as to the eye. She should be as narcissistic as an old-fashioned film star but she was disdainful of her looks. That wasn't to say she didn't make an effort with her appearance—she loved clothes, for example—but rarely did anything to enhance what she'd already been blessed with.

Anna Moretti née Robson, the woman with the face and body of a goddess and the tongue of a viper. Clever and conniving, sweet and lovable; an enigma wrapped in a layer of mystery.

He despised her.

He missed having her in his bed.

Since his release from prison all those long years ago he'd become an expert at masking the worst of his temper and channelling it into other areas, but Anna could tap into him like no one else and make him want to punch walls while also making him ache with need to touch her.

She wasn't a meek woman. He'd understood that at their very first meeting. All the same, he'd never have believed she would have the audacity to walk back into this building after the stunt she'd pulled.

'I'm not drunk.' He leaned closer and inhaled. There it was, that scent that had lingered on his bed sheets even after copious washes, enough so that he'd thrown out all his linen and bought new sets. 'But if you're having memory problems, I know something that will help refresh it.'

Alarm flashed in her widened eyes. He didn't give her the chance to reply, sliding an arm around her waist and pulling her to him so he could crush her mouth with his own.

He felt her go rigid with shock and smiled as he moulded his lips to hers. If Anna wanted to play games she had to understand that *he* was the rule maker, not her. He could make them and break them, just as he intended to eventually break her.

The feel of her lips against his, her breasts pressed against his chest, her scent... Heat coiled in his veins, punishment turning into desire as quickly as the flick of a switch...

All at once, she jerked her face to the side, breaking the kiss, and at the same moment her open hand smacked him across the cheek.

'What do you think you're doing?' She wiped her mouth with the back of her hand, her tone half shocked, half furious. 'You're...' Her voice tailed off.

'I'm what?' he drawled, fighting to control his own tone. The potency of the chemistry between them had become diluted in his memories. He'd forgotten how a single kiss could drive him as wild as an inexperienced teenager.

She blinked and when she looked at him again the fury had gone. Fear now resonated from her gaze. The little colour she'd had in her cheeks had gone too. 'Stef...'

She swayed, her fingers extending as if reaching for him.

'Anna?'

Then, right before his eyes, she crumpled. He only just caught her before she fell onto the floor.

CHAPTER TWO

WHEN ANNA AWOKE in the sterile hospital room, her head felt clearer than it had all day. The heavy pounding had abated but now came something far worse. Fear.

She didn't need to open her eyes to know she was alone.

Had Stefano finally left?

The memory of their kiss flashed into her mind. In a day that had passed as surreally as if she'd been underwater, his kiss was the only memory with any real substance.

He'd *kissed* her. It had been almost brutal. A taunt. A mockery. The blood thumping through her at the feel of it had been the final straw for her poor, depleted body. She'd collapsed. And he'd caught her.

He seemed to think they were married. The hospital staff were under the same impression.

Swallowing back the panic clawing at her throat, Anna forced herself to think.

Her memory of the day might be blurry but she remembered snapshots of it. Stefano had carried her to his office sofa while shouting for someone to call for an ambulance. He'd travelled to the hospital with her. He'd been with her through all the prodding, probing and questioning she'd endured when she'd been awake and coherent enough to answer. He'd even come to the scan with her. If it weren't for the dark tension radiating from him she would have been grateful for his presence, especially since Melissa hadn't shown up.

Where on earth was she? It wasn't possible that she could be on a flight to Australia. She wouldn't have done that without telling her. No way. Besides, they lived together. Anna would have known!

Just what the hell was going on?

Never mind all the so-called marriage nonsense, which had to be some kind of elaborate hoax, but since when had Stefano hated her? They'd always sniped at each other and communicated through sarcasm but it had always been playful, with no sting intended. Today, despite his seemingly genuine concern for her health, it had been like having a Rottweiler guarding her with its teeth bared in her direction.

The door opened and the consultant from earlier stepped into the room, clipboard in hand. She was followed closely by Stefano.

Anna's heart rate accelerated and she eyed them warily. They had the look of a pair of conspirators. Had they been talking about her privately?

'What's wrong with me?' she asked.

The consultant perched herself on the edge of Anna's bed and smiled reassuringly. 'You have a concussion from your fall last night.'

'I don't remember the fall,' Anna said. 'My sister wrote it in a letter…have you got in touch with her yet?'

'Her flight hasn't landed.'

'She can't be on a flight.'

'She is,' Stefano chipped in. He was seated on the

visitor's chair just a foot from her bed, his stance that of a man who had every right to be there. Even if she were to ask for his removal, no one would dare touch him.

His break away from her bedside seemed to have done him good though as he'd lost the Rottweiler look he'd been carrying all day. He looked more...not relaxed, not happy exactly, but...pleased with himself.

'Melissa's taken a month's leave to go to Australia and celebrate your mother's fiftieth birthday,' he finished.

'That's not possible.' The stab of betrayal pierced her hard. 'She couldn't have done that. I'd know.'

'The chances are you *did* know,' the consultant said. 'Your scan has come back clear...'

'What does that mean?'

'That there's no bleeding on the brain or anything we need worry about in that regard, but all the evidence is pointing to you having retrograde amnesia.'

'Amnesia?' Anna clarified. 'So I'm not going mad?'

The consultant's smile was more like a grimace. 'No. But it appears you have lost approximately a year of your memories.'

Anna exhaled in relief. Amnesia she could cope with. There had been moments during the day when she'd thought for certain she was losing her mind. And then she remembered Stefano's insistence that they were married...

'Don't tell me I'm actually married to him?'

Now the consultant looked uncomfortable. 'You're on our records as Anna Louise Moretti.'

There was silence as the meaning of this sank into Anna's fragile head.

She didn't know what was worse. Being told Melissa

had gone to Australia to see their mother or being told she was married to Stefano. Discovering that there was life on Jupiter would be easier to comprehend.

She turned her head to look at the man who claimed to be her husband. His long legs were stretched out before him, his tie removed and top button undone. He was studying her with an intensity that sent little warning tingles through her veins. It was the look he always gave when he was thinking hard, usually when he was debating to himself whether he wanted to risk his money and reputation on a particular venture.

When Stefano chose to back a business he didn't hold back. He gave it everything. He thrived on the gamble but liked the odds to be in his favour. He liked to be certain that he wasn't going to be throwing away his time, resources and money. It didn't matter how many reports she produced, he would play it all out in his mind, working through it on his own mental spreadsheet.

And now that gaze was directed at her, as if she were a business venture that needed to be analysed. He was mentally dissecting *something* and that something had to do with her.

'We're really married?' she asked him.

A slow smile spread across his face as if she'd said something amusing but the focus in his eyes sharpened. '*Sì.*'

None of this made sense. 'Why would I have married you?'

He shifted his chair forward and leaned over to speak directly into her ear. His warm breath stirred the strands of her hair, making her pulses stir with them. 'Because you wanted my body.'

His nearness meant she had to concentrate hard

to form a response. 'This is no time for your jokes. I wouldn't marry you. I have self-respect.'

He sat back and spread out his hands. 'No joke. We're married.'

'I don't believe you.' The very idea was preposterous.

'I can give you proof.'

'We can't be.'

There was no way she would have married Stefano. He was gorgeous, funny when he wasn't being brooding and impatient, and rich, but he also had a revolving door of girlfriends. She had always maintained that she wouldn't touch him with a ten-foot bargepole and had told him so on numerous occasions.

Always he'd responded with a dazzling grin and, 'You can't resist me for ever, *bambolina*.'

To which she'd always replied with her own grin turned up to full wattage, 'Watch me.'

This time there was no comeback. He pulled out his phone and started tapping away. After a few moments he leaned over to show her the screen. Her pulse made another strange leap at his closeness and the familiar scent of his tangy cologne that had always filled their workspace. She blinked and focused her attention on what he was showing her.

It was a photograph of them standing together on a beach. Stefano was dressed in charcoal trousers and a short-sleeved open-necked white shirt. She wore a long white chiffon dress that had a distinct bridal look to it, and was clutching a posy of flowers. Oh, and they were kissing.

Anna stared at the screen for so long her eyes went dry. Her heart was pounding so hard its beats vibrated through her. When she dared look at him she found him watching her closely.

'Did you drug me?' She could hardly believe the evidence before her. It wasn't possible. It had to be fake.

'We married on the twentieth of November. Our first anniversary is in ten days.'

'That's impossible.' She did some mental maths. She remembered as far back as her Spinning class, which had been the day after bonfire night, November the fifth.

He expected her to believe she'd married him two weeks later? Did he take her for a complete idiot?

But then she looked again at the photo on his screen.

'We married in Santa Cruz,' he supplied. 'It was a very…I can't think of the word, but it was quick.'

'Spontaneous?'

'That's the word, *sì*.'

Despite the mounting evidence she still couldn't bring herself to believe him.

'If we're married, why did I wake up in my own bed in mine and Melissa's flat?'

There was only the barest flicker of his pupils. 'We'd had a row.'

'About what?'

'Nothing important. You often stay the night there.'

'Why were you so angry to see me in the office this morning? And why has Chloe taken my desk?'

'I told you, we'd had an argument.'

'Cheating on me already?' she asked, only half jesting.

There was a tiny clenching of his jaw before his handsome features relaxed into the smile that had always melted her stomach. 'I've never cheated on a woman in my life.'

'You've never stayed with a woman long enough *to* cheat.' Stefano had the attention span of a goldfish. He thrived on the chase, growing bored quickly and moving straight onto the next woman to catch his eye.

'We've been married for almost a year and I've never been unfaithful,' he stated steadily.

'Then what were we arguing about?'

'It was nothing. Teething problems like all newly-weds deal with. You weren't supposed to be in this week so Chloe's been working at your desk.'

The image of the blonde woman following him out of his car popped back into her mind. She had no memories of that woman but the way she'd reacted to her, the way her already tender stomach had twisted and coiled, made her think she *had* met her. 'Who was that woman in your car this morning?'

Before he could answer, the consultant coughed un-subtly. Anna had almost forgotten she was there.

'Anna, I appreciate this is hard for you. There are a lot of gaps in your memory to fill.'

She sucked in her lips and nodded. A whole year of memories needed to be filled. A *whole year* that she'd lost; a big black void during which she had married her boss and Lord knew what else had occurred. 'Will I get my memories back?'

'Brain injuries are complex. There are methods that will help retrieve the memories, things we call "joggers", which are aids to help with recall, but there are no guar-antees. The country's top specialist in retrograde amne-sia will be here in the morning to see you—he'll be able to give you more information.'

Anna closed her eyes. 'How long do I have to stay here for?'

'We want to keep you under observation for the night. Providing there's no further issues, there's no reason you can't be discharged tomorrow after you've seen the specialist.'

'And then I can go home?'

But where *was* her home? Was it the flat she'd shared with her big sister since she was fourteen? Or with Stefano?

The nausea that had eased with the help of medication rolled back into life.

She couldn't have married him. Not Stefano of all people.

'You'll need to take it easy for a few weeks to recover from the concussion but your husband's already assured me he'll be on hand to take care of you.'

'So Stefano knows all this? You've already discussed it with him?'

'I'm your next of kin,' he said, his thick accent pronouncing 'kin' as 'keen', something that under ordinary circumstances would make her laugh. Right then, Anna felt she would never find anything funny again.

'No, you're not. Melissa is.' Melissa had been her next of kin since her sister had agreed to take sole guardianship of her when she'd been only eighteen and Anna fourteen.

The uncomfortable look came back to the consultant's face. 'Anna, I understand this is difficult for you but I can't discharge you unless you have somewhere to go where you will be looked after, for the next few days at least. Your husband is your next of kin but you don't have to go with him. Is there anyone else we can call for you?'

Anna thought hard but it was hopeless and only made her head start hurting again. The only person she was close to was Melissa. They both had friends—lots of them—but it was only each other that they trusted. Their friends were kept on the fringes of their lives and there wasn't a single one she could impose herself on for however long it took to be deemed safe to care for herself.

But Melissa was on an aeroplane flying to the other side of the world to visit the woman who'd abandoned them for a new life in Australia with a man she barely knew.

The betrayal sliced through her again, tears burning in her eyes.

'Anna, your home is with me.'

She closed her eyes in an attempt to drown out Stefano's hypnotic voice. She wished she could fall into the deepest sleep in the world and wake to find the normal order of things restored.

The sad truth was there was no one else who could take her in or, if there was, she couldn't remember them.

Whatever was wrong with her head though, wishing for something different wouldn't change a thing. Her world might be all topsy-turvy but this was her reality now and she needed to deal with it. Bawling her eyes out and burying her head in the sand wouldn't change anything.

She looked directly at him. 'I don't remember it being our home. I don't remember a thing about us other than that you're my boss and the bane of my life, not my husband.'

Was it her imagination or was that satisfaction she saw glimmer in his eyes?

'I will help you retrieve the memories. I don't deny our marriage can be…what's the word? Like many storms?'

'Tempestuous?' she supplied, fighting the urge to smile.

'That's it. We are very tempestuous but we're happy together.' He straightened his long frame and rolled his shoulders before flashing his irresistible smile. 'I need to get back to work and get things arranged so I can care for you like a good husband should. I'll be back in the morning for when the specialist gets here.'

He handed a business card to the consultant. 'If you have any concerns, call me.' Then he leaned over and placed the briefest of kisses on Anna's lips. 'Try not to worry, *bellissima*. You're the most stubborn woman I know—your memories won't dare do anything but come back to you. Everything will feel better once you're home.'

The endearment, *bellissima*, sounded strange to her ears. The most endearing term Stefano had ever used towards her before had been *bambolina*, Italian for little doll, which he'd thought hilarious. He'd often said he would mistake her for a princess doll were it not for her blunt tongue.

Anna watched him stroll from the hospital room, the good, faithful husband leaving to sort out his affairs so he could dedicate his next few weeks to caring for his poor, incapacitated wife, and all she could think was that she didn't trust him at all.

Until her memories came back or until she spoke to Melissa, whichever came first, she would have to be on her guard. She didn't trust Stefano any further than she could see him.

Stefano strode through the hospital entrance with a spring in his step. It was at times like this, when he had something to celebrate, that he wished he still smoked. But smoking was a habit he'd kicked a decade ago.

He was going to bring his wife home. The woman who'd used, humiliated, left him and tried to blackmail him was going to be back under his roof. He had big plans for her.

Those plans would have to wait a few days while she recovered from the worst of her concussion but in the meantime he fully intended to enjoy her confinement. Anna hated being fussed over. She was incapable of switching off, always needing to be doing something. Having to rest for a minimum of a fortnight would be her worst nightmare.

It cheered him further to know he would be there to witness her live through this horror.

Stefano intended to keep his word and ensure she was well-looked-after while back under his roof. He might despise her all the way to her rotten core but he would never let her suffer physically. He could still taste the fear he'd experienced when she'd dropped in a faint at his feet and knew he never wanted to go through anything like that again. It amazed him that she'd been able to get into his offices without collapsing, something the consultant had been surprised by too. If he hadn't been so angry at her unexpected appearance and unprepared for seeing her for the first time in a month, he would have paid more attention to the fact she'd looked like death warmed up.

Fate had decided to work for him.

Anna didn't remember anything that had happened between them. The whole of the past year had gone, wiped clean away. He could tell her anything and with her confined to his sole care and her sister on the other side of the world, there was no one to disprove it. Judging from the way she'd blanched when she'd learned Melissa had gone to Australia, she would be too angry to make contact with her any time soon.

All he had to remember was to keep his bitterness that she'd fooled him into marrying her inside. Anna could read him too well.

He'd called Melissa as soon as they'd arrived at the hospital, knowing Anna would want her sister there. He'd been put through to her boss and told that Melissa was on leave and had been planning her trip for months. Considering Anna had never mentioned it—and she surely would have done—he guessed Melissa had put off telling her for as long as she could. Certainly, when the two sisters had gone away for their trip to Paris, which *he* had paid for as a treat for his wife and which Anna had returned from early, determined to catch him up to no good, she hadn't known anything about it.

He found Anna alone in her private room flicking through a magazine, dressed in the same black jersey dress from the day before. She greeted him with a wary smile.

'How are you feeling?' he asked.

'Better.'

He sat down in the visitor's chair. 'You look better.' Then he grinned and ran a finger down her soft cheeks, causing her eyes to widen. 'But still too pale.'

She jerked her face away and shrugged. 'I slept but it was patchy.'

'You can rest when we get home.' The consultant had told him in private that the best medicine for concussion was sleep.

'I just can't believe I've lost a whole year of my life.' She held the magazine up. 'Look at the date on this. To me, it's the wrong year. I don't remember turning twenty-four. There are stories in here about celebrities I've never even heard of.'

'Once we get you home I'm sure your memories will start to come back.' But not too soon, he hoped. He had plans for his wife. 'Do you not remember *anything* about our marriage?' He wanted to make double sure.

'Not a thing. The last I remember you were dating that Jasmin woman.'

Jasmin had been the date who'd got food poisoning an hour before his scheduled flight to California for the industry tech awards. It had been her illness that had given him the chance to coerce Anna into attending with him in her place. It was only because it was far too short notice for him to get another date that she'd agreed. That, and the designer dress he'd had couriered over from the designer personally had helped make her decision. The awards evening had ended with Anna insisting the only way she would have sex with him was if he married her.

He didn't doubt her memories of their time together would eventually return. If anyone could bring them back, it would be his wife, the most stubborn, determined woman he'd ever met in his life. But in the meantime…

'Our marriage is a shock for you.'

'That's one way to describe it,' she murmured. 'I'd promised myself I would rather date a baboon than go on a date with you, never mind marry you. Have you really never cheated on me?'

He forced his tone to remain light through the blood roaring in his veins. 'Not once. We've had a few issues but nothing serious. We've been working through them.'

A few months ago he'd been pictured dining with one of his new Swedish directors, a blonde statuesque beauty he hadn't felt even a flicker of attraction towards. Anna had shrugged the ensuing press melee off but he'd known it bothered her. A second photo a fortnight later, this time of him dining with one of his female employees in San Francisco, had only added fuel to the fire. He'd explained his innocence, proving the picture had cropped out the other half-dozen employees also dining with them, and she had outwardly accepted it. But her distrust had grown and she'd no longer bothered to hide it. Her attitude had infuriated him so much he hadn't cared to explain that he liked socialising when he travelled abroad without her because it made the time pass so much quicker.

He should have known from that point that she'd wanted to catch him out just as much as the media had. She had wanted proof of his supposed infidelity.

Her hazel eyes were filled with the suspicion he'd become too familiar with. 'What kind of issues?'

'You've found it hard to be my wife. You don't like the media.' That much at least was true. Anna loathed being under the media spotlight. 'There have been many stories about our marriage being in trouble. If we were to believe the press we've split up a hundred times since we married. It is all poppycock. We married quickly. It is natural for us to have the teething problems.'

Her nose wrinkled. 'When you found me in your office it was as if you'd found the Antichrist trespassing. What was the argument about that made me sleep at Melissa's? Was it that woman I saw you with?'

Dio, even with amnesia her mind ran to suspicion. He'd already told her there was no one else. There hadn't been anyone else since they'd flown to California and their relationship had irrevocably changed.

'That woman you saw me with is my sister.'

'Oh. Sorry.' She looked shamefaced. 'I saw her getting out of the car after you and...'

'And you assumed I was having an affair.' She'd made that exact same assumption when she'd found Christina in their apartment. Finally she'd found the proof she'd been waiting for from the very moment they'd made their vows. If she'd bothered to ask for the truth he would have given it, but she hadn't cared for the truth. All she'd wanted was evidence of infidelity so she could bleed him for as much of his hard-earned money as she could get her grasping hands on.

He'd planned to reveal his sister in court, in front of a judge, so the law could see Anna's accusation for the entrapment it was. He'd looked forward to her humiliation. Now he had a different kind of humiliation in mind, one that would be far more pleasurable. If she retrieved her memories before he could pull it off then so be it. He would enjoy it while it lasted.

'Sorry,' she repeated. 'I thought you were an only child.'

'So did I until recently. I'll tell you about it when you're not so exhausted.'

On cue, she covered her mouth and yawned widely, then blinked a number of times as if trying to keep her eyes open.

'Lie down and rest,' he said. 'The specialist will be here soon and then we'll be able to go home and you'll be able to sleep as much as you need.'

As much as he despised the very air she breathed, seeing her vulnerable and weak sat badly inside him, made him feel strangely protective. It made him want to hold her close and stroke her hair until she fell asleep. He much preferred it when her wits were sharp. It put them on equal footing. Her amnesia was a weapon in his own arsenal that he would use to his advantage but he wouldn't unleash its full force until he was satisfied she was over the worst of her concussion.

She nodded and lay down, curling up in the foetal position she always favoured when she slept. After a few minutes of silence when he thought she'd fallen asleep, she said, without opening her eyes, 'What did we argue about that was so bad I spent the night at my flat?'

'It wasn't anything serious. It's still your flat too and you often stay there. We've both been playing games. We're both stubborn, neither of us likes to admit to being wrong, but we always make it up.'

'If it wasn't serious, why were you so angry with me yesterday? You were grumpy for most of the time in the hospital too.'

Typical Anna. When she wanted an answer to something she was like a dog with a bone until she got it.

'I was hurt that you rejected me. I didn't understand you had amnesia. I was out of my mind with worry about you. Worry makes me grumpy. I'm sorry for behaving like that.'

Her eyes opened, an amusement he hadn't seen for a long time sparkling in them. 'An apology and an admission to hurt feelings? Have you damaged your brain too?'

He laughed and leaned over to press a kiss to her cheek. She scowled at the gesture, which made him laugh more.

It was as if this Anna beside him had been reset to factory settings before marriage had even been mentioned between them.

'I know you have no memories of us. I have to be hopeful they will return.' But not too soon. Too soon and he wouldn't be able to fulfil the plan that had formed almost the instant the consultant had informed him that his estranged wife had amnesia.

Their wedding anniversary was now only nine days away. To celebrate it, he had a surprise planned for her that no amount of amnesia would ever allow her to forget.

CHAPTER THREE

ANNA GAWKED AS the driver came to a stop along the Embankment. She'd always been curious about Stefano's home, situated in a high-rise residential complex overlooking the Thames, which, at the time of building, had been the most expensive development in the world. So naturally, Stefano owned the most expensive apartment within it: the entire top floor.

The driver opened Stefano's door. Before he could get out she touched his arm, only lightly but with an instinctive familiarity she'd never used before. 'You could be telling me anything about our relationship. I can't disprove any of it. How do I know I can trust you?'

'In all the time you worked for me did you ever know me to lie?' he answered steadily.

'I never caught you out in a lie,' she conceded. In the eighteen months she'd worked for him their relationship had been nothing less than honest, brutally so on occasion.

'So trust me.' He held her gaze with that same intense look that sent tendrils of something curling up her spine.

'It doesn't seem I have much choice.'

If she could remember her phone's pin code she could reach Melissa and ask her but even if she could, she knew she wouldn't make that call. Not yet. The thought of speaking to her sister made her feel sick. She wouldn't call her until she could trust she wouldn't scream down the line at her and say things she knew she would regret.

She must have known about Melissa's trip. Melissa's letter had said as much. She'd asked for her forgiveness.

How could she forgive that? After everything their mother had done and put them through? Their father had been six feet under for less than six months when their mother had started seeing an Australian man she met through a dating agency. Anna, who'd been desperately grieving the loss of the father she'd adored, had tried to understand her mother's loneliness. She really had. She'd resisted the urge to spit in the usurper's tea, had been as welcoming as she could be, believing Melissa's private assertion that it was nothing but a rebound fling by a lonely, heartbroken woman and that it would fizzle out before it really started. If only.

Three months after meeting him, nine months after she'd buried her husband, Anna's mother had announced she was emigrating to Australia with her new man.

Stefano pressed his thumb to her chin and gently stroked it. 'When your memories come back you will know the truth. I will help you find them.'

Her heart thudding, her skin alive with the sensation of his touch, Anna swallowed the moisture that had filled her mouth.

When had she given in to the chemistry that had always been there between them, always pulling her to him? She'd fought against it right from the beginning, having no intention of joining the throng of women Stefano enjoyed such a legendary sex life with. To be fair, she didn't have any evidence of what he actually got up to under the bed sheets; indeed it was something she'd been resolute in *not* thinking about, but the steady flow of glamorous, sexy women in and out of his life had been pretty damning.

One of her conditions for accepting the job as his PA was that he must never ask her to be a go-between between him and his lovers. No way would she be expected to leave her desk to buy a pretty trinket as a kiss-off to a dumped lover. When she'd told him this he had roared with laughter.

When had she gone from liking and hugely admiring him but with an absolute determination to never get into bed with him, to marrying him overnight? She'd heard of whirlwind marriages before but from employee to wife in twenty-four hours? Her head hurt just trying to wrap itself around it.

Had Stefano looked at her with the same glimmer in his green eyes then as he was now? Had he pressed his lips to hers or had she been the one...?

'How will you help me remember us?' she asked in a whisper.

His thumb moved to caress her cheek and his voice dropped to a murmur. 'I will help you find again the pleasure you had in my bed. I will teach you to become a woman again.'

Mortification suffused her, every part of her anatomy turning red.

I will teach you to be a woman again?

His meaning was clear. He knew she was a virgin.

Anna's virginity was not something she'd ever discussed with anyone. Why would she? Twenty-three-year-old virgins were rarer than the lesser-spotted unicorn. For Stefano to know that...

Dear God, it was *true*.

All the denial she'd been storing up fell away.

She really had married him.

And if she'd married him, she must have slept with him. Which meant all her self-control, not just around him but in her life itself, had been blown away.

She'd taken such pride in her self-control after her mum had left. Events might fall out of her power but her own behaviour was something she controlled with iron will. All those teenage parties she'd been to when alcohol, cigarettes and more illicit substances were passed around and couples found empty spaces in which to make out... She'd been the one sitting there sipping on nothing stronger than a cola and taking great pride in the fact that she was in control of all her faculties. Her self-control was the only thing she'd *had* control of in a life where she'd been powerless to stop her father dying or her mother moving to the other side of the world and leaving her behind.

A different heat from the mortification ravaging her now bloomed as her mind suddenly pictured Stefano lying on top of her...

His eyes still holding hers as if he would devour her in one gulp, Stefano trailed his fingers down her neck and squeezed her shoulder. 'Let's get you inside. You must rest. You're exhausted.'

Anna blew out a long breath and nodded. For once she was completely incapable of speech.

She'd shared a bed with him.

She'd shared more than a bed with him.

Trying desperately to affect nonchalance, she had no choice but to allow him to assist her through the grand atrium of his apartment building to his private elevator. It was either that or have her unsteady legs collapse beneath her again.

She'd always been physically aware of him before but with his arm slung protectively around her shoulders that awareness flew off the scale.

The dividing line she'd erected between them and worked so hard to maintain... Noting Stefano's easy familiarity with her; the way he was so comfortable touching her now along with the flirting she'd long been used to... Yes, that dividing line had been demolished.

She just wished her body didn't sing its delight at his new proprietorial manner with her.

It was such a relief to be led to a sofa to collapse onto that it took her a moment, catching her breath, to take stock of Stefano's home.

Her home.

It was like stepping into another world.

She was sitting in a living room so vast and wide she felt like a toddler who'd stumbled into a ballroom, the room complete with a gold-leafed crystal chandelier gleaming magnificently above her.

Floor-to-ceiling windows covered the entire perimeter and from one aspect gave the most amazing view of the Thames—was that Westminster Bridge she could see in the near distance?

Not a single memory was jogged by any of it. She'd lived here for almost a year but she was seeing it for the first time.

She looked around wondering where everyone was. 'No staff?'

'I don't have staff. The concierge service runs my housekeeping for me and I pay them a fortune for it.'

When Stefano had first made his fortune in his home town of Lazio, he'd employed live-in staff but had soon learned to dislike having other people in his space.

Housekeeper, cleaners, butler, chef, gardener…the list had been endless. Being waited on hand and foot sounded fantastic in theory but in practice it was a drag and he'd put the staff on day-only duties within weeks.

He was a fully grown man who'd been caring for himself since he was fifteen. He didn't need someone to dress him or run his baths. He saw his peers with their homes full of enough staff to fill a cinema and thought them fools for allowing themselves to revert to infancy.

It was all the fawning he couldn't abide. That was one of the reasons he'd been so keen to employ Anna as his PA. She'd been completely unaffected by meeting him, a reaction he hadn't received in years. In a business setting he was used to fear being the primary reaction; in his personal life he received desire from women and enthusiasm from men, both sexes looking at him with dollar signs flashing in their eyes. Anna had looked at him with disdain.

He'd strolled into the Levon Brothers offices when they'd been in early discussion about him buying the business from them and she'd been behind the desk in the office guarding theirs. He'd handed her his coat as he walked past for her to hang for him and heard a sarcastic 'You're welcome,' in his wake. He'd paused at the door he'd been about to open and looked at her, standing with his coat in her arms, challenge set in her eyes, jutting chin and pursed lips.

'What did you say?' he'd asked.

'I said that you're welcome. I meant to say it in my head just as I'm sure your thanks for me taking your coat off your hands was said in *your* head, but it slipped out.'

It had been a sharp salutary reminder of the importance of manners, something no one had dared to pull him up on for many years and it had taken a scrap of a woman to do just that.

He'd put a hand to his chest, made a mocking bow and said, 'Thank you.'

She'd nodded primly and crossed the room to hang his coat on the stand. Shorter than the women who usually caught his eye, she had the most exquisite figure, perfectly proportioned. He remembered exactly what she'd been wearing that day, a billowing checked skirt that had fallen below her knees, long tan boots with spiked heels, a tight black vest and a fitted khaki-coloured jacket, all pulled together with a thick belt with studs that looked sharp enough to have someone's eye out.

'Do I dare ask if you make coffee?' he'd asked, fascinated by her.

'You can ask but beware—refusal often offends.'

Roaring with laughter, he'd gone into his meeting. Within an hour, when the beautiful, sarcastic secretary had been brought in six times to explain the report she'd compiled for him but which the idiots running the company didn't understand, he'd known he was going to buy the company and poach her to be his PA. It turned out Anna was the real brains behind Levon Brothers. Without her by their side and covering their messes, it would never have taken off. With her by Stefano's side, Moretti's could only strengthen further.

It had been the best business decision he'd ever made. He'd learned to trust her judgement completely.

He'd believed her to be as straight as a line. He'd thought that with Anna what you saw was what you got, when all along she'd been nothing but a grasping gold-digger.

Now the bravado that always shone in her eyes was muted by alarm. 'It's just you and me here?'

'We like our privacy,' he said. 'We can walk around naked without having to worry that we'll frighten anyone.'

Her cheeks turned the most becoming crimson but she raised a tired brow and wanly retorted, 'I can assure you I won't be walking anywhere naked within a mile of you.'

Amused by her stubbornness even when she was so clearly ready to fall into a dead sleep, he whispered into her ear, 'And I can assure you that when you're feeling better you will never want to put your clothes on. Believe me, *bellissima*, we spend a lot of time together naked.'

'If I don't remember it then it didn't happen.'

Studying the firm set of her lips, he remembered what it had been like between them when they'd first married. He'd had no idea she was a virgin until she'd blurted it out when they'd walked into the bridal suite hours after exchanging their vows. She'd stood as defiant as she did now but there had been something in her eyes he'd never seen in her before: fear. That had been a bigger shock than her declaration of virginity.

He'd made love to her so slowly and tenderly that night that when he'd felt her first climax he'd been as triumphant and elated as if he'd been the first man to conquer Mount Everest. That night had been special. Precious. And it had only been the start.

Once Anna had discovered the joy of sex she'd been a woman reborn and unleashed.

She had no memories of any of it. When he next saw her naked, for Anna it would be the first time, and he remembered how painfully shy she'd been then.

He took one of her hands and razed a kiss across the knuckles. 'Can you walk to the bedroom or shall I carry you?'

Her eyes flashed and she managed to inflect dignity into her reply. 'I can walk.'

She allowed him to help her to her feet and held onto his arm as he led her to the bedroom he'd slept alone in for the past month.

The last twenty-four hours had brought such a change to his fortunes that Stefano was tempted to wonder whether it was *he* who had suffered a bump to his head.

His wife was back under his roof and shortly to be back in his bed.

He caught her unconcealed surprise when he opened the door to reveal a room cast in soft muted colours and dominated by an enormous emperor bed.

'We chose the decor together,' he told her. '*You* chose the bed.' It had been the first thing they'd bought as a married couple. He'd known she would hate sleeping in a bed he'd shared with other women.

And now they would share it again. Anna needed to know that this was *theirs*, a bedroom they'd created together, a room they'd made love in hundreds of times. He needed to consolidate in her mind that they were a properly married couple and that it was natural for them to sleep together.

He couldn't begin to dissect his own feelings about sleeping by the side of the woman who had played him for a fool so spectacularly.

'Seriously?' she asked in a voice that had gone husky.

'*Sì*. And when you're better I can promise you'll enjoy it as we always used to. But all that can wait. Consultant's orders are for you to do nothing but rest for the next few days. I promised I would take care of you and you know I am a man of my word.'

He always kept his word. To his way of thinking it was what separated humans from animals. He'd married Anna giving his word that he would be faithful. He'd given his word that if he ever felt the impulse to cheat he would tell her before acting on it and they would go their separate ways.

She'd given him her word too. She'd promised she would trust him. Her word had been a lie. Her intentions had been a lie. It had *all* been a lie. Their entire marriage had been built on lies and deception. No sooner had she left him than she'd hit him with her demands for a massive slice of the fortune he'd built from nothing.

Anna was a greedy liar who had made a fool of him, and for that she would pay the price.

But however greedy and conniving his wife was, right then she was too wiped out for any games.

She slumped onto the bed and sat there blinking to try and keep her eyes open. He sank to his knees and unlaced her boots before carefully removing them, then got her settled and comfortable under the bed sheets. She was asleep before the automatic curtains had finished shutting.

His guts twisted as he took in the sallowness of her complexion and the dark hollows under her eyes. He fought his primal reaction to lean over and smooth the hair from her face and place a kiss on her cheek.

He closed the door on the darkened room. There was no place in their relationship for sympathy. Anna's amnesia and her current vulnerability did not change what she'd done to him. Nothing could change that.

Soon her concussion would pass and she would be physically fit again.

Then the games could commence in earnest.

When Anna next opened her eyes, her first conscious thought was that someone lay beside her.

Not *someone*. Stefano.

When had he come to bed?

She hardly remembered getting into bed herself her exhaustion had been so sudden and so complete.

Stefano had brought her to the apartment early afternoon. Judging by the absolute darkness shrouding her it now had to be the early hours of morning. She must have slept for a good twelve hours straight and she felt better for it. The nausea had gone and her head felt thick and fuzzy rather than pounding. Her throat was parched but even if she knew where the kitchen was she didn't dare move from the bed. She hardly dared to breathe.

That was Stefano lying beside her, sharing this bed. If she moved her foot it would brush against his leg.

Did he have clothes on? Or was he lying there naked...?

The only sounds were his rhythmic breathing and the thundering of her heart.

It was the strangest feeling in the world to be in such an intimate environment with him, especially after eighteen months of doggedly keeping their relationship on a professional footing. She'd spent more time with him than anyone else when their working lives had bound them together. They'd travelled all over the world together, eaten together, had the occasional drink together, sniped at each other, laughed at each other, laughed with each other, sworn at each other, thrown things at each other…yet she had never allowed him to cross the threshold into her private life and had steadfastly refused to cross the threshold into his. They'd never been alone as they were now.

And here she was. Married to him and wholly aware that during their marriage they had done far more than merely sleep in this bed.

Stefano awoke with an almost painfully obvious erection. In their marriage's previous life he would have pulled Anna into his arms and made love to her before either of them had opened their eyes. Today he jumped out of bed and took a shower before he could act on that urge.

While he'd told himself that it was no big deal sharing a bed with his wife again, he'd had to psych himself up to join her in it. That had been unexpected. He'd gazed at her sleeping form in the dim light and experienced the strangest combination of loathing and compassion sweep over him.

He'd never known Anna to be ill before. He'd never seen her vulnerable. He'd lain beside her unable to get out of his mind that she was there, in his bed, the place he had once believed she belonged. It had taken him an age to fall asleep.

As he lathered himself with his expensive shower gel, it occurred to him that this was the first time in a month he'd woken up feeling this kind of desire.

Celibacy was not a healthy state to live by and he could only assume it was his loathing for Anna consuming all his waking moments that had stopped him seeking another woman in the month since she'd gone. He hadn't even thought of another woman to warm his bed; no wonder he reacted so viscerally just to have her back beside him.

But he wouldn't act on it yet. Seduction of his wife would have to wait for now.

Anna was awake and sitting up when he returned to the bedroom with only a towel around his waist. He noted the way her eyes widened at his bare torso and smirked.

'Feeling better?' he asked. She looked better. Her face had regained its colour, although that could be due to embarrassment at his semi-naked form. This was the first time in her memories that she had seen him anything but fully clothed. He worked hard to keep himself in shape and she had made no secret of her appreciation of his body.

She jerked a nod and pulled the covers tighter. That she was still wearing the jersey dress she'd collapsed in two days ago only made her embarrassment more amusing.

He strode over the thick carpet to his dressing room. 'Can I get you anything? A cup of tea?'

Anna was addicted to tea. He'd once counted her drink nine cups in one day.

'Tea would be good, thanks,' she muttered.

'Painkillers? Food?'

'Just painkillers, please.'

Deciding not to torment her further by dressing in front of her, he threw on a pair of jeans and a black T-shirt in his dressing room, then went to the kitchen where her teapot and teabags still lived.

He automatically reached for her favourite morning mug, a vessel so large it could reasonably be classed as a bucket, and a fresh burst of fury lashed through him.

He should have got rid of all her possessions instead

of keeping them here as a constant reminder. He'd given in to his anger only the once since she'd left him, in their San Francisco apartment, and had despised himself for his momentary weakness. Since then, his fury had been internal, simmering under his skin, crawling through him, festering.

Anna's amnesia had given him the perfect means to channel his rage into something far more satisfying than making a bonfire from her belongings.

His rage was back under his full control when he took her tea to her and placed it on her bedside table.

'I've ordered a light breakfast for you,' he said, handing her the painkillers.

'I'm not hungry.'

'You need to eat something.'

Anna took the pills from him and pulled a face, but her retort about not wanting to eat died on her lips when she noticed his bare wedding finger. She looked at her own bare hand and asked, 'Why don't we wear wedding rings?'

'You didn't want to. You said it would make you feel like a possession.'

'You didn't mind?'

'It was a compromise. You agreed to take my name on condition of no rings.'

'I would have thought it would be the other way round and that I'd refuse to take your name,' she mused.

His smile was fleeting. 'You wanted to be a Moretti so when we have children we can all have the same name.'

'We want children?' That shocked her almost as much as learning she was married to him had.

He shrugged then flashed his gorgeous smile. 'At some

point. When we're ready. Until then we've been enjoying practising making them.'

Something poked in her memories, squeezing her heart and making her stomach clench so hard his unsubtle innuendo barely registered. Desperately she tried to capture the feeling but whatever *it* was fluttered out of reach before she could put her finger on it.

'What is it?' he asked, staring at her with drawn brows.

'I don't know.' She shrugged and shook her head. 'Not a memory. A feeling.'

'Good or bad?'

'Painful.' That was the only word she could think of to describe it. She'd always wanted children but it had been something shoved to the back of her mind, a 'one day' want. She'd imagined she would one day reach the stage where her biological clock started ticking furiously and then be forced to make her decision. And that would have been hard as she'd always avoided relationships. If her own mother hadn't loved her enough to stay, how could she trust any man to?

When had she looked at Stefano and decided she could trust *him*?

She'd been attracted to him from the first moment she'd met him but which woman wouldn't be? The outrageously handsome, infamous boss of Moretti's had strolled into her office as if he already owned the building and had arrogantly placed his coat in her arms without a single word of greeting, never mind thanks. When she'd sarcastically responded with, 'You're welcome,' to his retreating back, she hadn't cared about offending him. Being a woman in a heavily male-dominated environment had caused her to grow skin as thick as leather and she'd adopted an unwillingness to tolerate sexism

in any form. She'd known her worth to Levon Brothers
as well as they had. She'd merely been given the title of
secretary because her two bosses there had been too un-
imaginative to think of a more appropriate title. They'd
only been a few years older than her, a couple of eggheads with more brains than an elephant and less com-
mon sense than a dormouse.

Stefano had paused and turned to face her and in that
moment she had experienced a flicker of nerves at crossing some invisible line with a man with such a ferocious
reputation; a billionaire who'd come from nothing and
served time in jail, but then their eyes had clashed and
something else had flickered inside her. Attraction.

So attractive had she found him that she'd thought long
and hard before accepting his job offer. He'd assumed
she was playing hardball for more money and increased
his offer, but money had been the least of her concerns.
Stefano had a magnetism about him, a power that clung
to his tailored suits and the dashing looks of a matinee
idol. All this and the element of danger that oozed from
him had proven a potent mixture and one she'd been wary
of committing her working life to.

In the end, the pluses of taking the job had outweighed
the minuses. She had never regretted her decision. She enjoyed working with him. Even on those days when they'd
be working towards some deadline that would see them
in the office late in the evening, bad-tempered and shouting at each other, she had never regretted it. That she'd
spent most days fighting her own responses to touch him
or act in any way inappropriately was something she had
learned to live with. That Stefano seemed to know exactly
how badly she desired him was something she had sworn
to never give him the satisfaction of confirming.

So how had he worn her defences down enough to persuade her to marry him and consider having children together?

A ring vibrated through the apartment, startling her.

'That will be our breakfast,' he said.

'That was quick.'

'That's why I pay such a high price for the service.' He reached the bedroom door. 'You need to build your strength up, *bellissima*. I need you fit to fly in a few days.'

'Why? Where are we going?'

'California.' The smile he gave was unlike any she'd seen on his lips before. 'It's the industry awards next week. And our first wedding anniversary. Where better to celebrate it than where it all started?'

Stefano waited until he heard the shower running, then dialled the contact on his phone.

Anna had spent her second day in the apartment sleeping on and off. After her small evening meal she'd declared she needed a shower. Her health was improving by the minute.

His call was answered within two rings.

'Miranda, it's Stefano,' he said. 'How would you like the celebrity scoop of the year?'

CHAPTER FOUR

FOR THE SECOND night in a row Anna woke to darkness and the regular deep breaths coming from her right. The covers she'd burrowed under had been pulled down and the chill of the winter night covered her skin.

Holding her breath, she turned her head to look at him. Stefano slept with his back to her, the covers twisted around his waist. As with the night before, he slept deeply. She couldn't keep her eyes off him. Her heart seemed to make a clenching motion and the urge to rest her hand against his warm skin grew almost overwhelming.

Cautiously, she tugged at the sheets, trying to dislodge them without waking him. She managed to free a couple of inches, and tried again.

She didn't want to wake him. There was something about the darkness of night that heightened the intimacy being alone in his apartment evoked in her senses.

She would never have believed he could be so attentive. Nothing was too much trouble for him, not the endless cups of tea, the regular small meals...he'd even had a pair of pyjamas couriered to her from Selfridges. She was certain that if she were to wake him up and ask him for something he would do it without complaint. It made her realise that she must mean something to him as a wife, that he had true feelings for her. If only she could remember what her own feelings towards *him* were.

Eventually she came to the conclusion that she would have to wake him. It was either that or freeze.

'Stefano,' she whispered. When there was no response, she repeated his name, louder. Still no response.

She would have to touch him...

She took a deep breath, then quickly poked him in the back. 'Wake up. You've stolen all the covers.'

It was like arguing with a corpse.

After trying to wake him a few more times with minimal contact, she sat up. Now holding her breath, she put a hand to his shoulder and gave it a quick shake before snatching her hand away.

That did the trick.

He rolled over. 'What's the matter? Are you feeling ill?'

'You're hogging the bed sheets.' She lay back down and fixed her gaze to the ceiling, making sure to keep a good distance between them.

'Sorry.' He yawned widely then untangled himself and breached the small distance she'd created to pull the covers up to her shoulders. Then he settled himself back down next to her, on his side, facing her. A centimetre closer and he would be pressed against her. 'We decided long ago that you're a refrigerator at night and I'm a radiator.'

Going by the heat coming off him now she could believe it.

She swallowed and croaked out a reply that was nowhere near as witty or nonchalant as she wanted. 'I normally sleep with bed socks on.'

Bed socks were as unsexy as they came and right then

she was prepared to grab at anything that didn't make her think of sex.

He chuckled lightly, as if he knew what she was thinking. He was so close his warm breath whispered against her skin. 'You don't need them any more. We both sleep naked. I keep you warm.'

She tried to breathe but suddenly it seemed as if all the air had been sucked from the room. As hard as she tried to resist, her head turned of its own accord to face him.

A flame flickered to life inside her, turning her core to liquid. If she rolled over she would be flush against him.

Help her, she wanted to be flush against him. Her lips tingled to feel his mouth on hers again but this time for her to be coherent enough to savour the moment.

As if he could sense her silent yearning, Stefano breached that last, tiny distance and brushed his lips to hers in the softest of caresses.

And then he pulled away and rolled over so his back was to her again. 'Go back to sleep, *bellissima*.'

Anna only just stopped herself from crying out. She clamped her lips together and lay there rigidly, waiting for her heartbeat to return to its normal rhythm and the flames still flickering inside her to subside.

If they weren't married she would be plotting her escape from this dangerous situation where the biggest peril was herself. Yet somewhere in her past, in the blank space that was her memories, Stefano had worn her defences down. She'd acted on the desire she felt for him.

And now, God help her, she wanted to act on it again.

Anna managed to fall back into a light sleep, a restless state where her body didn't know if it was awake or dreaming. Stefano seemingly had no such problems, sleeping deeply while she lay fidgeting, her mind a whirl, questioning everything: her marriage, her sister's betrayal... When six o'clock finally struck she decided to get up.

Physically, she felt a lot better. Almost normal. Her legs had lost the jelly-like feeling she'd been experiencing every time she stood and the ache in her head was now a dull thud rather than rivalling a pneumatic drill.

Tiptoeing over the thick carpet so as not to wake Stefano, she opened her dressing-room door and closed it quickly behind her so the light wouldn't disturb him. It was the first time she'd entered this room.

She experienced another in a long list of surreal moments. Floor-to-ceiling fitted white wardrobes lined the walls, while at the far end of the room sat a vanity desk, a full-length mirror and a squishy armchair. And it was all hers.

She opened the nearest door and found a row of trousers and jeans. The next door opened to display a row of tops. As she fingered the expensive material of a silk green and black checked shirt that caught her eye, a memory flickered, a sudden image of herself in this very room looking at herself in the mirror wearing this very top.

It was the first concrete memory of her missing year since she'd woken three days ago.

Stefano woke to a bed he knew was empty before he opened his eyes. Through the duration of their marriage he'd become accustomed to waking next to Anna, usually with their arms and legs entwined. He'd learned as a teenager to sleep anywhere he could rest his head but nowhere did he sleep as deeply or as sweetly as when Anna lay beside him. He hated that fact about himself.

He shrugged on his robe and went in search of her. He found her in the kitchen looking through a drawer, dressed in her favourite green and black checked shirt and a pair of slim-fitting dark grey canvas trousers. Her hair was brushed and pulled back in a loose ponytail and on her feet were the fluffy duck slippers he'd bought as one of her birthday presents. He'd chosen them as a joke but of all the things he'd bestowed her with on that day, which included a surprise holiday to the Seychelles, the slippers had been her favourite.

He'd spotted a pair of fluffy lamb ones only a week ago and his first thought had been to buy them for her as an early Christmas present. A split second later he'd remembered that Anna no longer lived with him and the only Christmas present she would receive from him would be his contempt.

'It's good to see you up.' He hooked an arm around her waist, dropped a kiss on the nape of her neck and inhaled her delicious soft floral scent.

Turning his back on her in the early hours of the night had been hard but necessary. He'd sensed her desire simmering beneath her rigid surface and known that with only a little persuasion on his part she would be his for the taking. But it was too soon for her. When he seduced her anew, he wanted his wife to be a tinderbox of desire for him. He wanted her to beg for his possession. He wanted her helpless to do anything but melt in his arms. He wanted her fully fit and knowing exactly what she was doing.

The more heightened her emotions and desire for him, the greater the low that would follow when he exacted his revenge.

She stiffened but didn't pull away or shrug him off.

He pressed one more kiss to her neck and stepped back.

'What are you looking for?'

She cleared her throat but kept her back to him. 'My phone charger. I can't find it anywhere and yours doesn't fit into my phone.'

'You probably left it at the flat.' There was no probably about it.

'Can we go and get it?'

'Sure. What do you need it for?'

She turned her head and cast him with a glance that contained a trace of amusement. 'To charge my phone, obviously.'

Oh, yes, she was definitely on the mend.

Then her amusement turned to a scowl and she flung the phone to one side. 'I guess it doesn't matter if I get the charger when I can't remember the pin code to get into it. Do you know what it is?'

'No.'

'Can I use your phone?'

'What for?' he asked cautiously.

'I want to call Melissa.' There was the slightest tremor in her voice. 'You must have her number.'

'I do,' he admitted. It was pointless to lie. If Anna was determined to speak to her sister she would find a way. His job at this point was to deter her. 'Are you sure it's wise to speak to her yet?'

'I want to know why she's gone to visit our mother... unless you can tell me?'

'Her decision to go was very sudden,' he said, thinking quickly. 'I shouldn't speculate what her reasons were.'

'I only want to know why she's gone. You say you're

my husband—this is the sort of thing a husband would know.'

'I *am* your husband, Anna, but Melissa's reasons are hers alone. I don't think you should contact her until your memories return. If they come back to you before she gets home from Australia then you will know the truth for yourself. If they haven't come back by then, the two of you can sit down and you can hear her reasons from her own mouth.'

Her eyes flashed with anger. 'Our mother abandoned us to live with another man when our dad wasn't even cold in his grave. I don't want to wait for a month to know why Melissa's suddenly decided to forgive her.'

Stefano strove to keep his features neutral. Anna must assume he already knew all this but he'd only known the basics about her mother's emigration to Australia. The way she'd always spoken about it was that staying in England to live with her sister was something they'd all been happy about and that the two sisters' estrangement from their mother had grown organically over time, a simple result of living on opposite sides of the world.

He didn't want to know any more. She'd had a year to confide her secrets to him but had chosen to keep them to herself.

Stefano held no truck with traumatic childhoods. His own was there for the world to see. He wasn't in the least ashamed of his past but could think of nothing worse than sitting down to dissect its effect on him. The only effect had been to act as fuel for his success.

He didn't want to know anything more about his wife than he already did. He didn't want to delve into her psyche and would not allow her to delve into his.

That chance had long gone.

He took her hands in his and brought them to his lips. 'I know you find Melissa's actions painful but all that matters is getting your memories back. Everything will fall into place when they return.'

She held his gaze, the ire slowly evaporating from them until she sighed. 'It's not just Melissa. Or you. I feel so out of the loop with everything. I was watching the news earlier and there's so much happening in the world I know nothing about.'

It was only eight o'clock. 'How long have you been awake?'

'A couple of hours. I've had so much sleep that I'm all rested out.'

'You should have woken me.'

'I knew you'd say that. And I did think about it but, other than my head aching a little, I feel normal. It would have been mean to wake you. Besides, you sleep like the dead.'

'Fed up of being fussed over?' he teased.

The wry smile broadened and she sniggered. 'Fed up and bored rigid. There's not even any housework for me to do. Everywhere is spotless.'

'I knew it wouldn't take long for you to get bored,' he said smugly. 'But I have a cure for your boredom. Let's fly to California tonight. The sun and change of scenery will do you good and being there might act as one of those joggers the specialist spoke about.'

California was where she'd reeled him in like a fish on a hook. It was only fitting he did the same in return.

Her face suddenly brightened. 'I did have a memory come to me when I was in my dressing room. Nothing significant, just a memory of wearing this shirt.'

A sharp stabbing struck at his brain. 'It's your favourite,' he confirmed, forcing his features to relax. 'And that memory must be a good sign.'

'I hope so,' she said reverently. 'It's a start in any case.'

'It is. So do I tell my crew they're taking us to California today?'

She thought for a moment then nodded. 'Do it. It can only help me.'

'I shall make the call now.'

'Aren't we going to San Francisco?' Anna asked when Stefano's driver took them down a different highway from the route she remembered. She'd travelled with him on business to San Francisco a number of times, stopping at a hotel while he would stay in his penthouse apartment.

He grinned. 'Your amnesia means I get to surprise you twice.'

'What do you mean?'

'You'll see.'

They'd landed on a sunny late afternoon. The Californian warmth felt wonderful on her skin, the majestic redwood trees lining the route as they wound through the mountains...

'Are we going to Santa Cruz?' she asked as they drove past a sign with the name of an approaching town she recognised. She'd gone for a hike in the summer through the Forest of Nisene Marks State Park on her day off during a week spent in the Moretti's San Francisco building.

'You'll see,' he repeated. He took hold of her hand and brought it to his lips to breathe a kiss across the knuckles.

She snatched it away. 'Can you stop playing games for two minutes and give me a straight answer?'

Although she'd slept for most of the flight, her body thought it was the early hours of the morning, not the early Californian evening they'd landed in. It was driving her crazy that he wouldn't give her a straight answer to anything, not even their destination.

He cast her with hurt eyes that didn't fool her for a second. 'I like to give you surprises.'

'Don't give me that. You're on one of your power trips. You're loving having me at your mercy.'

'I don't have the power trips.'

'But you don't deny that you love me being at your mercy.'

His voice dropped to a murmur as he leaned close to speak in her ear. 'I love nothing more than having you at my mercy, *bellissima*. And you love it too.'

'And you can stop with the innuendoes,' she snapped. 'You're supposed to be helping me get my memories back. All you're doing is alluding to sex. Is that all our marriage amounts to?'

'It's the best part of it.'

'Well, from now on you can take it as read that I know we have a fantastic sex life.' She could feel her cheeks burn as she spoke but refused to allow herself to be distracted. 'So I would appreciate it if you would remember that I know nothing of our life together and am relying on you to fill the holes—and if you make an innuendo out of that I shall get a flight straight back to London.'

His lips twitched and he settled back and folded his arms across his chest. 'What do you want to know?'

'Where we are going for a start!'

Right on cue, his driver took them over the border into the hip, arty city of Santa Cruz.

'We're going to our beach house,' he confirmed. 'We bought it a few months ago. This is the city we got married in.'

Slightly mollified, she said, 'Why did we marry here?'

'California allows quick marriages. I told you to name your city. You chose Santa Cruz.'

'*I* chose? You didn't frogmarch me to a register office?'

'Marriage was your idea.'

'I don't believe you.'

He shrugged. 'It's the truth. You flew to San Francisco with me as my guest for the awards ceremony. At the end of the evening I got my driver to drop you at your hotel first.' He spread his arms. 'We had our first kiss in this car. Things got a little…hot but you wouldn't let me come to your room. I asked what it would take to get you into my bed and you said marriage.'

'I must have been joking.' She *must* have been. Anna had never even thought of marriage, had assumed she would grow into a grey-haired spinster surrounded by dogs—not cats—and had been comfortable with that. Singledom was safe. It wasn't men specifically that she didn't trust, it was people. People were selfish. People put their own needs and wants first. They broke hearts and left others to pick up the shattered pieces.

'You said you were.' He shrugged again and in the movement she thought she glimpsed a darkening of his features that passed so quickly she guessed she'd imagined it. 'But the idea took hold with both of us. I came back to your hotel in the morning knowing I was going to marry you that day. It was what we both wanted.'

'But *why*?'

'We wanted each other and we'd both reached our limit of you keeping me at arm's length. Think about it, *bellissima*—what couple was better suited to marry? We'd worked closely together for eighteen months. We'd seen the worst of each other. We'd fought. We spent more time together than with anyone else but we never quit. If a man and a woman could truly be friends then that's what we were.'

'You're my boss. I'm paid to be nice to you.' But even as she made the jest she was wondering where love had come into it. That was why people married, wasn't it? Because they trusted someone enough to give them their heart as well as their body? It was why she'd never thought *she* would marry.

He snorted with laughter. 'When did that ever stop you saying what you think of me? We married knowing exactly what we were getting into. It made perfect sense.'

And as Stefano finally explained how he'd worn her defences down, a warm feeling spread through her.

For all their sniping at each other in the workplace, they'd forged a strong camaraderie. A bond. She would attend meetings with him, sit in on interviews for both staff and acquisitions, travel the world with him... She'd got to know him so well she would know his opinion on a person or situation before he'd opened his mouth to vocalise it.

She'd learned that though he was an exacting task-master, his word was his bond. She might even have learned to trust him.

Suddenly she could see exactly why she'd married him.

Not only was he the sexiest man to walk the planet, but by marrying her Stefano had proven he wanted her as more than just another notch on his endless bedpost.

Love must have been a gradual progression between them. It appeared Stefano was wisely avoiding talk of it knowing it was pointless to talk of love with someone who had no memory of it. His pride must be so hurt with it all, she thought, feeling a twinge of compassion for him, having to be the one to hold her steady until her memories of the life they'd forged together returned; having to trust that they *would* return and that she would remember all they'd meant to each other.

'I can see how it happened,' she said quietly, nodding slowly as she processed it all. 'But I must have asked for some kind of reassurance that you would be faithful. Your track record with women hardly inspires confidence.'

If he hadn't been such an unashamed womaniser she might have given in to her desire for him sooner. There had been nights when she would lay awake aching for him, filled with pent-up frustration that working so closely with him brought. Day after day of breathing in his scent, watching his throat move while he ate and drank, catching a glimpse of exposed torso when he'd rip his constricting tie off or a glimpse of his forearms when he'd roll up his sleeves... She had become obsessed with those arms. She would dream about them. She would dream about him.

'Your only request was that I tell you if I met another woman I wanted to bed so you could walk away with your dignity intact. It was a promise I was happy to make.'

'It's good to know I didn't completely lose my marbles.'

'You did,' he assured her solemnly but with a glint in his eye. 'I told you I would wear you down eventually and I was right.'

'You're always right.'

'*Sì.*'

'In your own head.'

Catching his eye again, Anna suddenly, inexplicably, found herself unable to stop laughing.

'What's so funny?' he demanded to know.

'Everything.' She covered her mouth with her hand, trying hopelessly to regain some composure. 'You must be an amazing kisser if one kiss in the back of a car was enough to make me marry you.'

The wolfish gleam in his eyes and the way he leaned closer made her suddenly certain that he was going to show her exactly what it had been like, right here and now.

She waited in breathless anticipation for his mouth to press on hers.

But then he grinned and the moment was lost. 'We're here.'

CHAPTER FIVE

ANNA SNAPPED HERSELF back to the present. They'd entered a private enclave lined with clean wide roads fringed with palm trees.

As they got out of the car, the salty air of the Pacific and its accompanying breeze filled her senses, along with a tremendous sense of déjà vu. She *knew* this place.

The house they'd stopped outside was stunning, a modern Spanish-style beach home that, from the outside and despite its grandness, looked surprisingly cosy.

Cosy was a word she'd never used in association with Stefano before.

She followed Stefano through the front entrance and into a home that made his London apartment seem like a shoebox.

'Take a look around. I'll get us a drink.' He disappeared through an arch and into the kitchen.

Intrigued by her surroundings, she trod her way through the ground floor, over marble floors, under high ceilings, soft furnishings and elegant decor. The only room accessed by a door was a cinema with a dozen plush leather seats.

Carrying on with her tour, she found an indoor swimming pool, a gym, a majestic dining room… She finally came to a stop at the rear of the house. The glass walls overlooked a palm-tree-lined patio area and another swimming pool, which in turn overlooked a glorious sandy beach and the deep blue Pacific. On the left of the room was the most enormous rounded sofa she'd ever seen, almost bed-like in its proportions.

'You said this is ours?' she asked in amazement when he joined her a short while later holding two tall glasses of fruit juice.

'*Sì.*' He handed a glass to her. 'I would have poured us champagne but it's not a good idea for you to drink alcohol until you're fully recovered from your concussion.'

She raised a brow. 'How do you know I'm not?'

'Because I know you, *bellissima*. I don't want to rush you. When you're fully better we can celebrate.'

'Celebrate what?'

'You being here.'

She couldn't know what a truth that was. Stefano wasn't about to tell her that they hadn't spent a night together under this roof, that the purchase had been finalised three days before she'd left him. Especially as part of the settlement she'd instructed her lawyer to hit him with had been a demand for this house. Now he would taint the memories of it for her as much as she had tainted them for him. Here, in this house that was supposed to have been their first real home, the one they'd chosen together, he would seduce her so thoroughly that all the pleasure they shared would haunt her for ever. Her humiliation would be twofold: public *and* private. Just as his had been.

Her cheeks coloured. She cleared her throat and took

a sip of her juice, then looked around again and said conversationally, 'You like your glass walls, don't you?'

'What do you mean?'

'Your apartment in London has external glass walls. Is there a theme?'

'I don't like to be...what's the word when things are too near to you?'

'Hemmed in? Cramped?'

He shrugged. 'Both could be it. I like space and light. I had enough of being cramped when I was a child.'

'You weren't put in a cupboard under the stairs, were you?' she asked teasingly.

'I spent a year living in a cellar.'

Anna eyed him warily, unsure if he was joking. Everyone knew of Stefano's torrid childhood—he wore it as a badge of honour: the teenage drug-addicted mother who died when he was a toddler, the teenage drug-addicted father who'd disappeared before he'd been born, the grandfather who'd raised him until his own death when Stefano had been only seven at which point he'd been sent to live with a succession of aunts and uncles. He'd always been fighting and causing trouble and being kicked out to live with the next family member until there had been no family members left willing to take him in. From that point on he'd been alone. At the age of fifteen.

He'd spent years begging and fighting to make a living, finding work wherever he could in the seedy underbelly of Lazio's streets. At the age of nineteen, to no one's surprise including his own, he'd been sent to prison but, within a year of his release, the adolescent who had been expected to spend his life as a career criminal had formed the technology company known to the world as Moretti's and the rest was history.

This was all public information. Stefano was happy to talk about his formative years with the media, proud of being the bad boy who'd made a success of himself.

As a PR strategy it had worked fantastically well, capturing the public's imagination and adding an edgy aura to the Moretti brand. It had the added advantage of actually being true, or so Anna had always assumed. Stefano's past crossed the divide from professional to personal so she'd never asked him anything about it other than in the most generic terms. Well, not in her memories in any case.

'Really? A cellar?'

'That was when I lived with my Uncle Vicente. My cousins there wouldn't let me share their rooms.'

'They made you sleep in a cellar because they didn't want to share?'

'They were scared of me—and for good reason. You do not keep kicking a dog and not expect it to bite. I was an angry teenager who liked to fight.'

Fighting was the only answer Stefano had had. A patchy education had left him severely behind at school, which, coupled with always wearing threadbare clothes either too big or too small, had made him a target for bullies. Once he'd realised he could silence the taunts from cousins and school friends alike by using his fists he'd never looked back. A volatile temper and a rapidly growing body had quickly turned him into the boy everyone crossed the road to avoid.

'Were all your family afraid of you?'

'They were when I hit puberty and became bigger

than all of them. I wasn't the skinny kid they could bully
any more.'

'Why did they bully you?'

'My mother was the bad girl of the Moretti family and
brought shame on them. I was guilty of being her son.
They only took me in because it was my *nonno*—my
grandfather—his dying wish. They hated me and made
sure I knew it.'

'That's horrible,' she said with obvious outrage. 'How
can anyone treat a child like that? It's inhuman.'

'It makes you angry?' he asked with interest.

'Of course it makes me angry! If Melissa had a child
and anything should happen...' Her voice faltered and
she blanched at the weight of her own dark thoughts. 'I
would love that child as if it were my own.'

Yes, she probably would. If his wife was capable of
loving anyone it was her sister.

She shook her dark hair and took a drink of her juice.
'Do you ever see them now?'

'You know I don't...' But then he remembered she
knew nothing of the last year and how all their time not
working had been spent in bed. When they'd been only
boss and employee she had determinedly made a point
of asking him little about his free time. 'The last time I
spoke to any of them was when my Uncle Luigi turned
up when I was still living in Italy asking for money. My
answer would make a nun blush.'

Her face broke into a grin and she laughed. 'I can
well imagine.'

'Do you know, I walked out of my Uncle Vicente's
house—was kicked out for breaking my cousin David's
arm in a fight—thinking of only one thing. Revenge.
I would make such a success of myself that my fam-

ily would have to see pictures of my face everywhere they went and read details of my wealth and know they would never get any of it. Whatever they did with their lives, I would do better. I would earn more money, eat better food, live in a better home, drive a better car. My success would be my revenge and it was. Everything I gained only drove me to get more.'

His revenge had fuelled him. The cousins who had begrudged him the clothes they'd outgrown, the aunts who'd begrudged feeding him, the uncles who'd treated their pets with more respect than they had their orphaned nephew... None of them would see any of his hard-earned gains.

'If the success you've had is any measure, your thirst for revenge must have been huge.'

Almost as great as his thirst for revenge on his wife.

He kept his voice steady as he replied, 'I am not a man to forgive. I forget nothing.'

Anna sat on the sofa, tucking her feet under her bottom and wishing she could put a finger on the danger she felt herself in. She kept her gaze on Stefano and was met with a sparkling gaze and the curve of his lips, yet there were undercurrents to this conversation that she was missing. She could feel it. A darkness, like a shadow that only showed itself intermittently.

'How did you do it?'

'I told people I was eighteen and found jobs on building sites and in clubs... Work was easy to find and working in the clubs meant it was easy to find a woman and a bed for the night.'

'When you were *fifteen*?'

'I didn't look fifteen. Women like a bad boy. I saved as

much as I could earn. I'd saved ten thousand euros when I was sent to prison and lost it all in legal fees.'

'What did you go to prison for? Fighting, wasn't it?'

'I saw a man in one of the clubs I worked at hitting a woman.' He raised his shoulders. 'I stopped him.'

'You beat him up?'

'He deserved it. He was two times her size. She couldn't defend herself. It was one of many fights I had in those years.' His smile was wry. 'The man I beat up that time was a policeman's son who made sure I went down for it.'

'Was prison really awful?' she asked tentatively.

He pulled a face. 'The worst thing was probably the food. Then the boredom. I had quite an easy time compared to many people but when I left I knew I would never go back. It gave me the focus to change. No more fighting.'

'What about the bedding of beautiful women?' she tried to say in a joking voice.

He pulled another face that quite clearly said she was pushing her luck.

If the thought of him bedding others didn't make her chest contract she would laugh.

'I had a little money left. I took it to a casino.'

'You gambled your savings?'

'A hundred euros. That's all I had left. If I lost it, I would have earned it back the next day and started again but I had a feeling... Like... Like...' His face scrunched as he tried to think of the word, and Anna was reminded that his English was entirely self-taught.

'Do you mean you had a gut instinct?'

'*Sì*. That's it. I played it on the roulette table and I won. I won big. I went outside for a cigarette...'

'Since when do you smoke?'

'I haven't for years but I did then. There was another guy out there. He told me about this app he'd designed to track mobile telephone devices. Apps were babies then. Smartphones were babies compared to now. I didn't understand it but I understood that he did. It was a risk but I'd won that money and decided on one last gamble. I put one hundred euros in my pocket and handed the rest to him. We wrote an agreement on a napkin. Two months later he found me and gave me back my investment plus the interest we'd agreed on. For me, it was the start of everything. Smart technology was my future. I didn't know how to develop it for myself but I'd proved I could spot a winner. I backed the brains and reaped the rewards.'

'You've always seemed so confident and knowledgeable about the technologies you invest in,' she said with bemusement.

'That first deal made me one of the first people to see their full potential. I would say I got lucky but luck had nothing to do with it. Instinct and hard work were what got me where I am.' He grinned. 'The best deal I ever made was investing forty per cent in developing that social media site. I made seven billion dollars when it floated on the stock exchange.'

'I remember that.' It had happened before he'd bought Levon Brothers and she'd begun working for him. 'Have you gambled again since that night? In a casino?'

'Gambling is for morons.'

She laughed and drained her glass. 'Your revenge must taste very sweet.'

'It does. Like strawberries and cream at Wimbledon.'

Another burst of laughter escaped her but there was

anger underlying it. 'I'm glad. Your family don't deserve anything after the way they treated you.'

'If they had treated me better, do you think they would have deserved something then?' he asked.

'That's not what I meant,' she protested. 'Your money is yours. You earned it, you're the only one with a right to it. If you choose to share it with anyone then it's that—a choice, not an obligation.'

'You don't think you're entitled to a share of it as my wife?'

'Of course not.'

His eyes burned intensely. 'But say we were to go our separate ways, would you not be tempted to sue for a large share of it?'

'No. And if I know you at all I would gamble my own money that you made me sign a prenup.'

For a brief moment his lips pulled together and his jaw tightened but then his features relaxed. 'We married too quickly for that.'

'So I'm not the only one who lost their marbles, then?'

That made her stomach settle a bit, knowing whatever madness had caught them in its grip to compel them to marry had been mutual. She'd always known Stefano had worked like a lion to build his fortune and enjoyed the fruits of his spoils like a sultan. Until that moment she'd thought she'd understood it but she'd underestimated him. The fight and grit it must have taken for him to build what he had was mind-blowing and her respect for him only grew.

Stefano finished his drink and smiled tightly. 'I think we both went a little mad that day.'

It was an insanity he would never allow himself to fall into again.

Anna put her empty glass on the coffee table. 'Has getting your revenge helped?'

'Naturalmente.'

'But has it helped you emotionally? You had such a lot to deal with…'

'It's over,' he interrupted with a shrug. 'I dealt with it at the time and moved on.'

'That's a lot to deal with and you were so young.' Her pretty eyebrows rose disbelievingly. 'I thought I'd been dealt a crummy hand but at least I've always had Melissa.'

Stefano flexed his fingers. He didn't want her sympathy or attempts to delve into his mind.

Anna's actions had hit him in a place his family had never reached.

'We make our own luck and fortune, *bellissima.* The past stays where it is.'

'I'm not so stupid that I don't know my dad's death and my mum's desertion affected me,' she said stubbornly.

'Are you calling me stupid?'

'Of course not. I'm just saying that I don't see how your revenge could have been enough…'

'It was more than enough.' He could feel his ire rising. Anna was the only person who dared speak back to him. They could argue and shout at each other like a pair of wildcats.

Those arguments had always made him feel so alive even before the days when they'd settle cross words in bed.

'We've had a long flight and you're exhausted. Rest for a few hours and then I'll order some food.'

She got to her feet and folded her arms across her

chest. 'Do you always brush me off like this now I'm your wife?'

'I'm not brushing you off; it's just not a subject worth wasting my breath on.'

Seeing her face turn mutinous, he forced a more conciliatory tone of voice. 'Let's not have an argument when we've only just arrived. Come, I'll show you the rest of the house.'

Anna stepped into a bathroom on the second floor with an external wall made entirely of glass.

'I've been in here before,' she said, the words popping out of her mouth as that feeling of déjà vu hit her again, all residue of their almost-argument forgotten.

This memory was more than a feeling though. This one had substance.

She hurried to the glass wall and looked out.

Just as she'd known, the bathroom jutted out over the sunroom on the ground floor giving an immaculate view of the ocean and their strip of private beach.

Excited at this burst of memories, she faced him. 'I remember this! This glass...you can't see in from the outside, can you?' She pointed to the free-standing bath. 'I remember saying how brilliant it would be to have a bath in here and watch the ocean. I *remember*.'

'I didn't think a bath would act as a jogger,' he said drily but with a stiff undertone that made her look at him.

He'd come to stand beside her. His face was inscrutable as he gazed out. 'Are you remembering anything else?'

Her excitement diminished as more longed-for memories stayed stubbornly stuck in the void. 'No.'

'More will come. I don't think it will be long.'

'I hope so,' she said fervently. 'It's so frustrating. You're going to have to fill me in on everything about work if they don't come back soon.'

'Forget work.' He gathered a lock of hair that had fallen onto a shoulder and smoothed it off her neck. 'I don't want you thinking about it until we return to London.'

'I can decide for myself what I think, thank you.'

'Your beautiful mind is one of the many things I adore about you.' He placed his other hand on her neck and gazed down at her. 'But all I want is for you to get better. I'm thinking of you, *bellissima*.'

'I *am* better.'

'Almost.' He stepped closer and inhaled. 'You're almost there.'

CHAPTER SIX

'DO YOU MISS ITALY?' Anna asked some hours later. She'd had a three-hour nap in their four-poster bed, which even had muslin curtains, then a shower, and gone downstairs to find Stefano had ordered Italian takeaway for them.

Now they were sitting outside on the terrace, the roar of the Pacific their music.

'I miss the food.' He removed the lid of one large box to reveal a sharing platter of antipasti.

'What about everything else?'

He thought about it. 'I miss speaking my language.'

'Your English and Swedish are excellent and your Japanese is pretty good too.'

'Is not the same. When I speak my language I don't think about the words before I say them. Is natural for me.'

'Okay, so that's the food and the language. Anything else?'

'Our summers are better than in London.'

She gave him the stern look with one raised eyebrow that she'd often fixed him with when she'd worked for him.

'I am Italian. I will always be Italian. It is in my blood and when I retire I will move back there.'

'You? Retire?'

He laughed. 'When I get to fifty I will stop working and enjoy what I have built for myself.'

She smiled. The soft hue of the patio lights lent her face an extra glow that only enhanced her natural beauty. If Stefano didn't know of the poison that lay behind the beautiful façade, he would be entranced.

'I can live with retiring in Italy.'

He made his lips curve. 'You've said that before but I think you will find it hard not to have your sister on the doorstep.'

Her smile faded into a grimace, pain flashing in her eyes. 'I think so too. I want to stay angry with her but it's too hard. She's my sister and whatever's happened between us I still love her.' She blew a puff of air out and shook her head. 'I need to speak to her.'

'You'll be able to soon. She's only away for a month. You two will sort it out, you always do.' As close as the two sisters were, they often argued. Some days Anna would hear her phone ring, see Melissa's name on it and say, 'I'm not in the mood to talk to *her*,' with a scowl. Other times they were quite capable of spending two hours on the phone, their conversations only coming to a close when one of their phone batteries ran out.

It came to him that when he went ahead with his plan to humiliate her at the awards ceremony she wouldn't have her sister to turn to.

Before his conscience could start nagging at him about this, he opened the bottle of wine he'd placed on the table and poured himself a healthy glass.

Anna stared from him to her own glass and the jug of iced water he'd put beside it, her nose wrinkling.

With equal parts amusement and irritation, he watched her pour herself some wine.

'You shouldn't be drinking.'

She rolled her eyes. 'One glass isn't going to kill me.'

'You have to be the worst-behaved patient.'

'You've lived with me for a year. That shouldn't be news to you.' She took a chunk of focaccia and dipped it in the *pinzimonio* before popping it into her mouth whole and devouring it with relish.

It was the first time she'd eaten anything with enthusiasm since her injury.

Suddenly he remembered all the meals they'd shared together and her love of good food. Anna had an appetite that belied her petite figure. This wasn't the first sharing platter they'd had between them, and when she picked up a tooth pick to swipe the largest bite of Parmigiano Reggiano before he could take it, the boulder that had been lodged in his throat settled in his chest.

'I've never known you to be ill before,' he said.

'Melissa says it's like caring for an adolescent toddler.'

He laughed at the mental image this provoked.

'I haven't taken a painkiller all day,' she pointed out. 'And speaking of sisters, you never did tell me how yours found you. Her name's Christina?'

'*Sì.* Christina. She reached out to me when our father died.'

'So your father was alive all this time?'

He nodded with a grimace. 'All those years I thought he was dead he was living in Naples, not even a two-hour drive away. I even had his name wrong—I always believed he was called Marco but it was Mario.'

'How awful.' Her hazel eyes were dark with the same

empathy he'd seen in them earlier. 'He was so near to you all that time? Didn't he want to see you?'

'He wasn't allowed.' There was little point in evading the subject. Anna had that look about her that meant she would chip away until she had all the answers she desired. It was what made her so good at her job: that refusal to leave any stone unturned. 'My *nonno* paid him to leave Lazio before I was born. He blamed him for my mother's addiction. My father took the money and ran, then he grew up and got himself straight, got a job and a place to live. He tried to get in touch with my mother and learned she had died. Nonno didn't trust him and told him to stay away from me. Rightly or wrongly, he agreed. He didn't trust himself any more than Nonno did but he did stay clean, met another woman and had a child with her—Christina. His wife encouraged him to get in touch with me directly but by then Nonno had died and I'd been kicked out by the rest of my family and living on the streets. He couldn't find me.'

'But he looked?'

'He looked, *sì*, but at that time I often used different names and I never gave my real age. He was searching for someone that didn't exist.'

'What about when you started to make a success of yourself?' she asked with wide eyes. 'Did he not realise it was you, his son?'

'He knew,' Stefano confirmed grimly. 'But he thought I wouldn't want to see him; that I would think he only wanted to claim me as his son to get some of my fortune.'

All those years he'd blithely assumed his father was a no-good junkie who didn't want him. But he *had* wanted him. His father had wanted to put things right. And now it was too late and he would never know him and never be able to tell him that he forgave him. His parents had been little more than children when they'd conceived him, and immature, addicted children at that.

While they'd been talking, they'd cleared the antipasti so all that remained were the pickled vegetables neither of them particularly liked.

'My father left me this watch.' He rolled his sleeve up to show it to her.

She looked at it with a pained expression, taking in the shabbiness of the leather strap and the scratches on the glass, then looked back at him. Her smile was tender. 'At least he died knowing you'd made a success of yourself. That must have given him comfort.'

He nodded and took the lids off their main courses, biting back the sudden anger that rushed through him that she could act so supportive now, when her platitudes were worthless.

Christina had given him a letter written by their father. He'd said Stefano had made him proud.

He'd never made anyone proud before.

He served the *linguine con le vongole* onto Anna's plate. She beamed. 'That's my favourite.'

'I know.' He served his lemon sole onto his own plate and took a bite.

Anna, who was a real pasta lover, twisted some linguini onto her fork, stabbed a clam, and asked, 'When did you learn all this?' before popping it into her mouth.

'A month ago.'

He'd learned the truth about his father while Anna was away with Melissa in Paris, the night before she'd flown back early and stormed into his boardroom to accuse him of having an affair. And he'd thought treating

Anna and her sister to a few days away together would be a good thing!

She'd called and left a message but he'd spent most of the night with Christina, talking and steadily making their way through numerous bottles of wine. He hadn't seen Anna's message until he'd gone to bed at four in the morning; too late to call her back. Then, with hardly any sleep, he'd had to get his heavy head to the office, leaving his new-found sister in the apartment.

While he'd been reeling over the discovery of a grown-up sister and a father who *had* wanted him, Anna had flown home early with the sole intention of catching him with another. Why else would she have come back, armed with accusations, without leaving a message of warning?

He'd been fool enough to think she cared when all she'd ever wanted from him was his money.

They ate in silence for a while before she asked, 'What's Christina like?'

'Very young, not long turned twenty but young for her age and very sheltered.' He pushed his dark thoughts about his beautiful wife to one side and smiled wryly. 'Reading between the lines, our father was afraid to let her out of his sight in case he lost her as he lost me. But we're building a relationship.'

'Has she been staying with us?'

'No.' Anna, damn her, was the only person he'd ever been able to stomach living with. 'I've rented a flat for her in London and she's doing some work experience at the office.'

'She doesn't have a job?'

'She'd just started her second year at university when our father was diagnosed with cancer. They thought they had more time so she arranged with the university to take the year off and return next September. Until then, she's going to stay in London and work for me and improve her English.'

'What about her mother?'

'She's in Naples but will be coming to London at Christmas.' Seeing Anna open her mouth to ask another question, he said, 'How's your meal?'

As with the rest of his life he had no qualms about discussing it but Anna had this way of listening that made him want to talk about more than the facts, to lay bare everything living under his skin.

It was an unburdening he'd fought to escape from in their marriage and he was damned if he would do it now when their relationship was days away from being over for good. The only unburdening he wanted from her was her clothes.

Anna was ripe for seduction, just as he wanted.

If he took her into his arms there would be only the slightest resistance. He could see it in the eyes that undressed him with every hungry look.

But something still held him back from acting on it. Whether it was the hint of vulnerability that still lingered in her eyes or the wine she'd been drinking when she really shouldn't so soon after her concussion he couldn't say, but, either way, not even his deplorable conscience would allow him to act on his desire yet. When he made love to her again he wanted to be certain that it was the Anna he'd married he was making love to. The vulnerability was almost gone. Almost. And when he was certain she was as well as she could be then, and only then, would he seduce her into an ecstasy she would remember for the rest of her life.

'It's beautiful, thank you.'

He raised his glass. *'Salute.'*

'What are we drinking to?'

'To us. You and me, and a marriage you will remember for ever.'

Anna's belly was comfortably full. It was the only comfortable part of her anatomy.

They'd long finished their meal and the bottle of wine and now sat, Stefano's eyes burning into her while she waited almost breathlessly for him to suggest they go to bed.

Heat flowed through her veins as her imagination ran amok wondering what it would be like, what it would *feel* like, to be made love to by him. To have that hard, naked chest she pictured every time she closed her eyes pressed against hers...

'Earth to Anna,' he said, elbow on the table, cheek resting on his hand, a gleam in his eyes that made her wonder if during their marriage he'd developed the power to read her thoughts. 'What are you thinking that makes your eyes glaze over like that?'

He flirted with her, he was tactile, he left her in no doubt he couldn't wait to bed her again...but so far he'd made no real move on her.

Was he waiting for her assent?

When she'd woken up three mornings ago feeling as if she might die, she'd had no idea that she was married. No idea that she'd shared a bed and her body with someone, let alone him.

Stefano was the only man she'd ever fantasised about. The only man she'd ever wanted. Her brain might not remember what he did to her but her body did. It ached for him with an intensity that made her bones liquefy.

And she was married to him! At some point in her past she'd found the courage to confirm her desire for him, both in words and deed.

She took a breath and looked him right in the eye. 'I was thinking that it's time for bed.'

He returned her gaze then slowly nodded. 'Go ahead. I'll join you later.'

She wasn't quick enough to hide her dismay. 'Aren't you coming with me?'

His eyes flashed before he closed them and inhaled slowly. 'I'm not tired enough to sleep yet.'

But she didn't want to sleep and she was damned sure he knew that.

Stung at his rejection, Anna got quickly to her feet. 'I'll see you in the morning, then. Night.'

'Anna.'

She ignored him to dart away from the table, not wanting him to see the mortification she knew would be written all over her face.

After all his innuendoes and hungry looks, he was rejecting her?

She couldn't escape from the terrace quickly enough.

'Anna,' he repeated in a voice that demanded to be obeyed.

Almost at the door, she reluctantly turned to face him. 'What?'

Under the soft glowing light she saw a knowing tenderness on his handsome face that took a little of the sting away.

'You're beautiful.'

His words were so unexpected that she found herself gazing from the simple blue shift dress she'd chosen from her enormous dressing room, slipping it on with thoughts of Stefano in her mind, to him, the man she ached to make love to.

Then he smiled wryly, poured himself another glass of wine and raised it to her. 'Sleep well, *bellissima*.'

The house was eerily silent when Stefano headed down the stairs the next morning wearing only his robe.

He found Anna at his desk in his office, his laptop open in front of her.

'What are you doing?' he asked with an easiness that belied the impulse to slam the lid shut.

'Trying to hack into your laptop.' She didn't look at him, and nor did she look or sound the slightest bit penitent at what she was doing.

'You can't get into your own phone. What makes you think you can hack into this?'

'Because you're extremely predictable with what you use as your password.'

Stefano had always given her free access to his laptop when she worked for him and he'd trusted her with his often-changing passwords for it. Of course, he only used it for work purposes and it was for this reason he didn't want her getting into it now. It would take her all of a minute to discover that he'd sacked her and then all his plans would come tumbling down. Everything would come out and the revenge he was working so carefully towards would be ruined.

He ignored the nagging feeling in his guts that it might just be a good thing for his plans to be ruined. 'What do you want it for?'

'To get onto the Internet.'

'Why? To email Melissa?'

'I agree with you that I shouldn't speak to her yet but she must be worrying that she can't get in touch with me.'

'If she's worried she'll contact the office. They'll tell her where we are.' And then Melissa really would have something to worry about. She knew all about their vicious split.

All he had to do was stop Anna contacting her for four more days.

Her eyes lifted to meet his. She scowled but not before he read the hurt on her face.

He hid his satisfaction.

She was still smarting at his rejection of her the night before. Declining her open invitation had taken a huge amount of willpower and he'd had to keep himself rooted to the chair to resist following her inside and up to the bedroom. *Dio*, he had wanted her so badly it was a physical pain. Now, in the cold light of day, he could hardly believe he'd been so selfless. Being selfless was not on his list of attributes.

There was no hint of any vulnerability in those flashing hazel eyes now. And she was stone-cold sober.

'Is something troubling you, *bellissima*?'

'No.'

He sat on the edge of the desk beside her, taking in the tight shorts and the coral T-shirt that caressed her small, beautiful breasts.

Her jaw clenched and she stabbed at the keyboard and hit return.

Suddenly her face brightened and she cast him with a wicked grin. 'I'm in!'

The grin fell when she saw what was on the screen.

It was a letter of termination he'd got Chloe to write for one of the men who worked in his development lab.

He'd been reading through it before he'd remembered a meeting he was supposed to be at. Forgetting a meeting would never have happened when Anna was running the place alongside him. He'd left the laptop open and had just arrived at the meeting when a breathless member of staff had run up to inform him that his estranged wife had barged her way into his office.

He'd closed the laptop without shutting it down on his return from the hospital and hadn't opened it since.

'You're sacking Peter?' she said, reading it quickly.

'He's been selling patent application details to one of our rivals.'

'You have proof of this?'

'Enough for me not to give him the benefit of the doubt.'

'Have you confronted him?' she asked suspiciously.

'We had a little chat.'

'Did I sit in on it?'

'It was just me and him. I wanted to give him the chance to confess. His behaviour in that meeting was very...what's the word? When someone can't sit still or talk properly?'

'Nervous? Jittery?'

'Both of those. His body language made his guilt obvious.'

'For heaven's sake, Stefano,' she exploded, sliding the chair back to slam against the wall. '*Anyone* hauled in for a private chat with you is going to act nervous and jittery. You can be terrifying and Peter is a nervous soul as it is.'

'Someone is selling secrets from that department. Too many things are being leaked and he's the only person it can be.'

'Maybe the system's been hacked!'

'Maybe we have a traitor in our team.'

'Who in their right mind would turn traitor on you?' Now she was on her feet with her hands on her hips. 'You're a terrifying ogre but on the whole you're a good person to work for. You pay extremely well and you're generous with perks—you've one of the highest staff retention rates in the industry! I *know* Peter. You hired him as a graduate only a couple of months after you hired me. He's as timid as a mouse but one of the brightest brains you've got, and he's *loyal*. Are you really going to sack him without concrete proof?'

'I can't risk keeping him on!' He conveniently forgot to mention that neither Peter nor any of his other staff or even his business had crossed his mind since she'd collapsed at his feet.

'Have you even looked into the possibility that one of your rivals has infiltrated the system?'

'Our system is foolproof as you very well know!' he shouted back.

'Rubbish! If even the Pentagon can be broken into then your system can be too. Do you want to ruin a life with no proof? Do you want to be sued for unfair dismissal?'

'No one has grounds to sue me.'

'Of course they do, you moron, if you treat them like this.'

'Now you're calling me a *moron*?'

'If the boot fits then wear it!'

This was what he'd missed in his month without her; someone to call him out and make him see things from a different angle. Everyone else was too damn scared to speak up.

Everything had gone wrong since she'd left him. He

couldn't think straight, too consumed with his anger and humiliation at her hands to think clearly.

Anna would never have let him meet an employee without a witness to report the unbiased facts and protect both parties.

That he had the highest staff retention rates in the industry was down to her. Sure, all the wages and perks were his to be proud of but with Anna gone there was no one there to fight the staff's corner, no counterbalance, no one to make him listen to reason.

This was just as it had always been between them, Anna thought through the blood pounding in her brain.

Stefano was facing her with the same angry stance she knew she must have, both of them glaring and snarling at each other until one of them backed down and apologised.

Except this time she was wearing only a pair of skimpy shorts and a tiny T-shirt, and he...

He was wearing a loosely tied dark grey robe with nothing underneath.

And then, without her knowing how she got there, she was in his arms, his mouth devouring hers, he was kissing her, she was kissing him, in the way she'd yearned to for so, so long.

Sensation such as she'd never known existed skipped over her skin and down into her pores. His tongue swept into her mouth, their lips dancing to a tune she hadn't known she'd already learnt, and she swayed into him, closing her mind to everything but the feelings firing through her.

This was everything she'd been dreaming of and more. His taste, his scent, the feel of his lips, the roughness of his stubbly jaw, the strength of his arms and the hardness of his chest crushed against her... It was heat in its purest, most carnal form.

He rubbed his cheek into her neck and clasped her to him. His other hand gathered her hair together into a sheath and roughly, yet gently, he pulled her head back.

'Now do you understand why we married?' he asked coarsely. 'That night we both drank more champagne than was good for us and I took advantage of it to kiss you, just as I did now, and you kissed me back.'

His hand holding her ground her to him.

She gasped to feel him huge and hard against her abdomen.

No wonder they'd married so quickly. If she'd felt even a fraction of the desire in that car as was swirling through her now...it was the headiest feeling imaginable. No wonder she'd demanded marriage. It was the only thing that would have a hope in hell of putting him off the idea and leaving her safe.

Yes! It wasn't a memory that came to her then but a feeling, a certainty that this was how it had played out.

She'd had no idea the attraction she'd held so long for him would turn her into fondue at his touch. She would have had to scramble to hold on to her sanity. But Stefano's own sanity had been scrambled too and he'd agreed to her flippant remark.

She didn't need to hold on to her sanity now.

They had made love many times in their marriage, and now she would get to experience it for the very first time all over again...

Fresh sanity suddenly struck her.

She didn't know what to do.

Stefano felt her hesitation.

Cupping her cheeks in his hands, he gazed deep into

her eyes and saw nerves merging with the desire, just as he'd seen the first time they'd made love on their wedding night, and with it he remembered that she had no memories of their lovemaking. None at all.

Sex was the only aspect of their marriage he had no doubts about. Clever little liar that she was, no one could fake those reactions. It had never been a case of going through the motions for a quick release but a real, deep connection that had scorched them both. He knew he would never find that with anyone else and he hated her for it; hated her for destroying his faith in what they'd shared.

For a few more days he could enjoy it all again but this, their first time together in over a month, was the first time for Anna. He had to remember that. When she'd confessed her virginity, although shocked, he could not deny his primal reaction had been elation that he would be her one and only.

'I'm not making love to you in here,' he said hoarsely before sweeping her into his arms.

She hooked her arms around his neck but the trepidation was still there. 'Why did you reject me last night?'

'Because I was waiting for my Anna to come back. When you shouted at me so passionately...' he kissed the tip of her nose '...I knew it was you.'

CHAPTER SEVEN

STEFANO SHIFTED HIS HOLD so she was secure in his arms and carried her up the stairs.

His Anna, he thought with a possessiveness that caught him off guard.

Only his.

But only for a few more days.

He couldn't think of that right now. Right now it didn't matter that the whole reason they were here was so he could seduce her so thoroughly that when he publicly ended things between them she had the added humiliation of knowing she had willingly lost herself to his touch and screamed out the name of the man who was playing with her all along. All he wanted at that moment was to sink himself into Anna's tight heat and lose himself in her.

The bedroom door was open, the bed sheets still unmade from the frustrated, tortured sleep he knew they'd both shared.

Something *more* had made him wait until he'd been certain she would be asleep before joining her, and it wasn't just that he'd wanted to be sure she was truly recovered and sober. It was that nagging in his guts speaking to him, putting doubts in his mind.

Now, having shared those searing kisses and felt her taut and hungry against him…

He laid her on the bed and in a moment had shed his robe and climbed on top of her.

Anna waited for him to kiss her again. He'd placed his hands either side of her head, his legs long and lean between her thighs, and he was staring at her…

He was staring at her as if he could eat her whole.

She thought of all the women that had been before her, those faceless women she had been desperate to keep away from, desperate not to know, terrified that if any of them were to meet her they would recognise the secret feminine signs of a woman in love. She had feared their pity. She had feared she would hate them for it. Now she was the one to pity them.

It wasn't possible that Stefano had looked at another with the hunger with which he was looking at her.

Stefano was hers. All hers. She would never share him with anyone.

How beautiful he was, as if sculpted in marble by a master and then injected with life. To feel him against her inner thigh, hot and ready, his own desire wholly evident even to a novice such as her…

Flames licked her everywhere.

She reached out to touch him again, pressing her hand to his chest, feeling the heavy thuds of his heart. She sighed and closed her eyes.

Never had she imagined his skin would be so warm and smooth to her touch, or that the fine dark hair that covered his chest would feel so silky. Slowly she trailed her fingers down to the hard muscle beneath the damp skin of his abdomen and heard his sharp intake of breath.

Still gazing at her, he took hold of her top and, with only the smallest movement from her, pulled it off.

His devouring gaze took in every inch of her but she was far too gone to feel any embarrassment. Her only moment of shyness came when he tugged her shorts down and exposed her most private area. Even that shyness flew away at his deep groan.

'*Dio*, you have the sexiest body,' he said in a pained voice. Then he brought his mouth back down on hers and she wound her arms around him and responded with all the passion alive in her heart.

Fresh heat enflamed her body, desire uncurling inside her, the yearning for Stefano's possession growing.

And as she rejoiced in all these wonderful sensations, she was jolted from the moment with a thought that had her turn from his hot mouth to gasp, 'What do we use for contraception?'

'You've had those injections since we got back from our honeymoon,' he muttered raggedly, hardly pausing for breath before his lips found her neck and her heart accelerated at the thrill racing over her skin and the burning in her veins, all worries of contraception happily dispatched.

Everything was heightened, all her senses were converging together. She started as she felt his mouth on her breast, then shut out the last of her nerves and succumbed fully to the pleasure being evoked in her every last cell.

His mouth and hands were everywhere, kissing, nibbling, stroking every inch, bringing her desire to a boil that was on the cusp of spilling over. Every touch scorched, every kiss burned and soon she wanted so much more than this heavenly torture. When his lips found hers again, she parted her thighs at the same moment he put a hand to them.

He muttered something, shifted, then took hold of himself and suddenly she felt him there, right at the place she most wanted him to be, and just as suddenly her fears returned and she froze.

Stefano must have sensed something wrong for he stopped what he was about to do and, the tip of his erection still poised in the apex of her thighs, stared intently into her eyes.

'There is nothing to fear, *bellissima*,' he whispered. 'Nothing at all. I would never hurt you.'

His lips came back down on hers and she returned the heady pressure of his kiss. As his tongue swept into her mouth she wrapped her arms around him then cried into his mouth as she felt him push inside her, so slowly and with such care that she could have actually shed tears.

But then all thoughts of crying were swept away because *he was inside her.*

All her fears were unfounded. There was no pain. She'd known in her head that there couldn't be, that her virginity was only in her head, but that sensible voice hadn't been enough to quell her anxiety that somehow her body would have forgotten along with her mind.

There was only pleasure. Deep, radiating pleasure.

In their time together Stefano must have learned exactly what she liked because the thrusts he was making inside her felt heaven-sent.

His movements increased, the groans coming from his mouth in her ear making the pulsations inside her thicken. She put her lips to his neck and inhaled his tangy, musky scent, driving him deeper and deeper into her.

The world became a distant blur, shrinking down to

just them and this magical moment. The secret torch she'd carried for him for so, so long had been lit into a furnace and all she could do was let the heat from it burn until it reached its peak and she was crying out his name, over and over, pleasure rippling through her in long waves.

Stefano gave a hoarse groan and drove so deeply inside her at his own climax that she wrapped her legs even tighter around him, wanting to savour every last bit of this incredible moment.

When he collapsed on her with his face in the crook of her neck, she held him tightly. She dragged her hands up the length of his muscular back and up to his head, threading her fingers through the thick dark hair. She could feel his heartbeat hammering in time to hers and thrilled to know that he too had felt the joy she had experienced.

'Is it always like that?' she asked when she had finally caught her breath. Dull pulses still throbbed inside her.

He gave a sound like a laugh and lifted his head. A smile played on his lips. 'Always.'

The next morning Anna woke up in her second strange bed of the week—the third if one counted the hospital bed—and stretched before turning her head to the sleeping figure beside her.

The early morning light illuminated him perfectly and for the first time she allowed herself the pleasure of gazing at Stefano without interruption from the doubts in her own head.

Making love to him had been beyond anything her imagination could have conjured up.

She covered her mouth to stifle the laugh that wanted to explode from her. If she'd ever imagined it to be even half as good as it had been she would have resigned on the spot. There was no way she could have dealt with working by his side day by day with those rampant thoughts.

The second time had been even better. And by their third time the last of her inhibitions had been vanquished.

Having got so little sleep she should be shattered but she wasn't. She had never felt anything like this, as if there were a beehive in her chest, all the worker bees buzzing to make honey inside her.

Climbing out of the bed carefully so as not to wake him—although, as she'd already learned, an earthquake would have trouble disrupting Stefano's sleep—she tiptoed naked out of the bedroom and walked to the bathroom at the other end of the landing.

She shut the door behind her and headed straight to the window to look out at the cerulean sky.

It was going to be a glorious day, she could feel it in her bones.

She ran the bath and added liberal amounts of bubble bath to it, then climbed in.

Doing nothing more than lying there in the steamy suds, she gazed out at the beach. In the distance she could see someone walking a small dog, the first signs of life in Santa Cruz. She wondered if she and Stefano had ever spoken of getting a dog. She'd had one as a child, a soppy cocker spaniel that had been as daft as a brush and as useful a guard dog as a packet of pasta.

An image came into her mind, so vivid that she bolted upright.

Making love to Stefano in their London apartment.

She hugged her knees, the image forming, becoming more than just a picture in her head. This was a memory, pure bona fide remembrance of them being together.

Anna had no idea how long she sat in that bath, her attention wrenched away from the view, thinking as hard as she had ever done, so hard her brain hurt. It wasn't until there was a tap on the bathroom door that she realised the bathwater had turned cold and the bubbles gone.

'Come in,' she called, startled out of her reverie.

Stefano strode in wearing nothing but a pair of white cotton boxers slung low on his hips and a sexy lopsided grin. His sleep-tousled hair swayed as he walked to her and crouched down to rest his arms on the side of the bath.

'You should be in bed.'

She raised a brow at him, her senses jumping in so many directions just to see him so that it took a moment to find her tongue. 'I'm remembering things.'

Stefano's stomach lurched.

He'd woken to an empty bed and with only one thought in his mind, namely finding his wife and dragging her back to it. In the middle world of sleep and waking, and distracted by the ache in his groin, this time *he'd* been the one to forget everything.

He searched her face carefully. There didn't seem to be anything dark or suspicious lurking in her clear gaze, only animation.

He allowed himself a small breath of relief. 'What are you remembering?'

'Us. Patches of us. Our wedding.' Her cheeks flushed with colour and she lowered her voice. 'Making love for the first time.'

'What are your memories of that?'

She palmed his face with her hand, a look of bliss spreading across her beautiful face. 'It was wonderful. *You* were wonderful.'

His chest filled with emotion. 'What else?'

'Business meetings. Did you promote me?'

He nodded. 'Nick retired. I gave the job to you.'

Her eyes widened. 'You put me on the board of directors?'

'Who else would I trust to keep the place running when I had to travel? You're an exceptional businesswoman—the whole board was behind your appointment. And not just because they're scared of me,' he added, before she could quip that they would back anything he said out of fear.

In hindsight he recognised that promoting Anna had been when their troubles had begun. As his PA she had travelled everywhere with him. As Vice President of Moretti's UK, second only to the US in his burgeoning technology empire, she had needed to be on hand in the UK when he travelled to America. They'd gone from seeing each other all day every day and sleeping together every night to spending up to a week apart at a time. That was when those insecurities had set in.

But she'd been—acted—insecure from the beginning, he reminded himself. Her accelerated promotion had only given her the tools to up her campaign.

Yet the wonderment ringing out from her eyes at this moment put more doubts in his head.

Anna was clever and stubborn. She could by turn be sweet then sour. She was good cop to his bad cop but people were always aware that her being good cop did not make her a pushover. If she thought someone was being an idiot she had no qualms about telling them so, just as she had no qualms about telling him. Until she'd hit him with that ludicrous demand for a hundred million pounds of his fortune she would have been the last person he'd suspect of being a gold-digger. The last person he would have suspected of having an agenda. He'd trusted her as he hadn't trusted anyone since his *nonno* had died and to discover it had all been a lie had shattered him in ways he couldn't explain even to himself.

Her fingers gently massaged his cheek. It was such a simple sign of affection but one that made his heart expand.

'I don't remember everything,' she whispered, bringing her face to his so the sweetness of her breath sighed against his skin. 'All that I remember of us as a married couple is spending long days in the office and long nights making love. I don't remember falling in love with you but I know that I did. I *know* I did. I can feel it as clearly as I can feel the bristles on your jaw where you need to shave.'

And then her eyes closed and her lips pressed against his, not moving, just breathing him in.

Stefano gripped the back of her head and held her tightly to him to deepen the kiss, his mind and heart racing.

She spoke of love? *Love?* That was a word neither of them had ever said before.

That was *not* what their marriage was about.

Then what was it about?

It had been about desire. The primal need for a mate. A partner. Someone to have *bambinos* with.

He had long wanted children. To have a child would be to ice the delicious cake that was his life. His hated cousins had an abundance of them, and he'd beaten them in everything except in the *bambino* stakes. But to have children he needed to find a woman to have them with and he hadn't trusted any of the women in his life with a vase, never mind a child. Still, he'd looked forward to seeing miniature versions of himself running around and causing havoc one day; a bloodline to pass his wealth on to.

He'd be damned if he'd leave anything to the other members of his family.

When he'd started making waves in the world of technology, and journalists had learned of his rags-to-riches background, the shady acquaintances of his early years, the prison sentence...suddenly they had wanted to interview him and hear his story from his own lips. He'd been happy to oblige, especially if it involved having his photo taken in front of his yacht or his private plane. Stefano had become a poster boy for the kids of Lazio, an icon to look up to, the local bad boy who'd turned out good. He didn't doubt for a minute that his family, who all still lived in the same homes in the same close-knit area he'd been dragged up in, knew everything about him. And he didn't doubt that his success made them sick.

See? he would say to them through the lens of the camera. *This is what you threw away. If you'd treated me like the orphan boy of your blood that I was and not like some kind of wild animal, these riches would have been yours.* He was Italian after all! Life and its riches were for sharing with family. But he'd decided when he was fifteen that he had no family. Everything he earned, every penny of it, was his and his alone.

When Anna had so flippantly—but trembling after that first passionate kiss they'd shared—declared that if he wanted to bed her he'd have to marry her, he'd known by the next morning that she would be the mother of his children. There was no one better suited. They worked fantastically well together, shared a chemistry that was off the charts and they already knew each other's faults. Marriage and babies together? Well, why not? If not her then who? At least life with Anna would be fun, he'd thought. And she was straight down the line. As sexy as a nymph. He'd trusted her. But love? Love was for romantic fools who needed to put a name to their desire rather than just accepting it for what it was: chemistry.

The only person who had ever shown him love or affection was his *nonno*. When he'd died, Stefano had quickly learned he was not a person to inspire affection. As he'd grown older and started catching the eye of beautiful women, he'd discovered lust but had known their desire for him was based solely on his physical attributes. If they could see him without the outer shell, they would be repelled.

Anna was the only person since his *nonno* to see beneath that shell and still want him. He had never repelled her. He'd infuriated her—yes, he could admit to that—but seeing the real man hadn't made her run. She was level-headed enough not to want to try to change him.

In her own way, she was a misfit like him. They'd understood each other as no one else could.

But then she'd so spectacularly accused, humiliated and dumped him and he'd realised that it had all been an act. What Anna had seen beneath his shell *had* repelled her but she had bided her time until she'd been in a position to go for the kill and take him for everything she could get.

Had she planned her scheme right from the beginning as he'd thought since that torrid black moment in his boardroom? Or had it formed over time…?

Things were getting confused in his head. He had to focus. He mustn't let what was happening between them now and her words of love cloud his judgement any further.

The feelings she was now mistaking for love were its opposite: hate. Only the utmost loathing of him could have made Anna do what she had done. If she'd felt even a flicker of love for him she would never have gone through with her grand plan.

And now he loathed her. *His* grand plan was coming together better than he could have hoped.

Stefano pushed the disquiet in his guts aside with force and concentrated on the desire blazing in his loins. He lifted her out of the bath and carried her wrapped in an enormous towel to their bed.

They spent the day making love but, during the spent times when they dozed, he couldn't shake the voice in his head telling him that his plan was in danger of un-ravelling.

Anna's dressing room in their Santa Cruz beach house was even larger than the one she had in Stefano's London penthouse. It took for ever to rifle through the racks of clothes, all of which still had their tags on. She guessed they hadn't spent much time here since they'd bought the house.

After much internal debate she selected a pear-green silk sleeveless wraparound dress that was cinched at the waist and fell like soft leaves to the knees, held together by a thin belt studded with dainty diamonds. She also earmarked a gorgeous red dress to wear to tomorrow night's awards ceremony.

Delving further into the shelves uncovered a shoe-lov-er's paradise and, after much consideration that involved trying on half a dozen pairs, she settled on sky-high beige diamond-encrusted mesh heels that she suspected she would never have been able to afford even if she'd set aside a whole month of her generous salary.

Stefano had never stinted on displaying his wealth. It seemed that same generosity extended to his wife, a thought that sent a pang through her chest. Four whole days in Santa Cruz, just the two of them, had revealed a side to her husband she had only suspected before. Not only was Stefano an amazingly considerate lover but he was considerate of *her*. It was the little things, like holding her hand to keep her steady when she got out of the swimming pool; taking her beach towel a long distance from her to shake the sand from it…all the little things that made her heart swell and made her rethink her original assumption that she'd lost her marbles by marrying him.

Marrying Stefano had clearly been the sanest thing she'd ever done. Their first anniversary was only days away, proof that they must have been happy together and that Stefano had kept his promise of fidelity. She just wished she remembered more than snapshots of it.

She must find an anniversary present for him. They were going to San Francisco tomorrow morning ahead of the awards ceremony. She'd see if she could sneak out and get him something there.

She checked her reflection one last time and left her dressing room.

She found Stefano hunched over the end of the bed reading something on his phone. He looked up as she entered.

His eyes gleamed and a slow smile spread over his handsome face. '*Bellissima*, you look beautiful.' Then his eyes drifted down to her feet. 'Should you be wearing shoes that high in your condition?'

'What condition?'

'You've had severe concussion,' he reminded her.

She waved his concern away. 'I feel fine...' But as she said the words something tapped at her, another of those sensations of déjà vu she kept experiencing.

Condition...

The image of an oblong stick with a small window flashed through her mind. 'Have I been pregnant?'

His brows drew together. 'No. What makes you think that?'

'I don't know.' She blinked and shook her head in an attempt to clear the image.

He got to his feet and stepped over to her. He put a hand on her shoulder, peering at her intently. 'Anna? Are you feeling okay?'

She nodded then shook her head again. This was awful. There was something in her memories screaming to escape but she was helpless to find it. All she knew with any certainty was that this memory was bad and the only thing soothing her heightening fears was the sensation of Stefano's hand against her bare skin.

She took a shaky breath. 'Are you *sure* I've not been pregnant?' She didn't see how she could have been if she had used the injectable contraceptive.

'Very sure. I told you we said we would try for a baby one day in the future. Are you getting memories of that?'

'I don't know what I'm getting memories of.' She sighed, loosening the panic that had been trying to crawl up her throat. 'Nothing's clear.'

'It will come. Give it time.'

'You keep saying that. What if they never come back?'

'They will.' His fingers slipped lightly over the shoulders of her dress and rested in the arch of her neck. His gaze didn't leave hers.

Her chest filled with a feeling that was tight yet also fluid, moving through her veins and into her limbs; she was intensely aware of his closeness and the sensations shimmering through her at his touch.

One touch and she was a slave for more.

She looped her arms around his neck. 'What time have you booked the table for?'

The best way to shake off the dark uncertainty that kept trying to cloud her was by making love. Stefano's touch drove all her fears away.

He laughed huskily into her ear. 'We're already late.'

CHAPTER EIGHT

THE RESTAURANT STEFANO had booked them into was a short walk from their home in the Westside of Santa Cruz. Anna adored the clean, affluent neighbourhood. This was a district to soak up culture, enjoy the amusements and raise children.

Why did she keep thinking of children? And why did it feel like a blade in the chest whenever she did?

She pushed the thoughts aside. This was their last night in Santa Cruz and she wanted to enjoy every last minute of it, not have her unreliable mind take her in directions she couldn't understand.

The Thai Emerald was, as the name suggested, a Thai restaurant, located on the bustling beachfront.

She glimpsed a small room with a handful of tables before they were whisked up narrow stairs to a bright, spacious room with an open front overlooking the beach.

They were shown to a small square table near the front and menus were laid before them. Their drink order was taken and then they were alone.

Anna read her menu with a contentment in her heart she couldn't remember feeling since childhood.

'You look happy,' Stefano observed with a smile.

She beamed at him. 'Thai food is another favourite.'

'I know.'

'Do we ever cook?'

'No.'

He answered so firmly that she laughed. 'Melissa always did the cooking and I did the cleaning...' Her voice tailed off as she thought of her sister.

'You are most particular about tidiness,' he said with a grin.

'Melissa says I'm a control freak.'

'You like order. There's nothing wrong with that. I'm the same.'

The waiter came to their table with their wine and poured them each a glass.

'I've been thinking,' Anna said once their food order had been taken. 'I'm going to get in touch with Melissa when we get back to London.'

'I thought you were going to wait until she got home?'

'I'll drive myself crazy if I wait that long.' She sighed. 'I miss her. I can't wait another three weeks to speak to her. I'll borrow your phone if that's okay and call her.'

He nodded thoughtfully. 'If you're sure.'

'I am. I just feel...' She shook her head. 'Betrayed. I know it's selfish of me but I want to know why. After everything Mum did to us, to up and leave to celebrate a birthday with her? I mean, she left us. She left me in Melissa's care when I was fourteen years old and scarpered to the other side of the world to live with a man she'd known for only a few months. What kind of woman does that? What kind of *mother* does that?'

How many times had he heard all this? she wondered when he didn't answer.

Her mother wasn't a topic Anna liked to discuss. It was the judgement call she could read in people's eyes when they learned about it, as if they were wondering what kind of daughter she must have been if her own mother abandoned her so soon after her father had died.

It was something that ate at her. What kind of hateful child must she have been to elicit that desertion?

But Stefano was her husband so it was only natural that in the course of their marriage she had opened up to him. And all he was doing right then was listening to a story she must have shared however many times but couldn't stop relaying again now.

'I often wonder what would have happened if I hadn't put my foot down and refused to go with her. I don't see how our relationship would be any different other than the fact I would have been on the other side of the world to my sister. Melissa couldn't have gone. She'd just started university and was starting her adult life. I didn't want to leave her or my friends. I didn't want to leave my father.'

'Your father was dead,' he pointed out quietly. 'Didn't you want your mother to be happy?'

'Of *course* I did but it was so soon; his death was so sudden.' Her father had been killed when a wall had collapsed on him at the building site he was a manager of. 'All my life it had been the four of us, a tight family unit... How could she have loved Dad if she started seeing Mick so quickly after burying him? How can you visit a grave when you're on the other side of the world?' She rubbed her eyes, only slightly aware that they were wet. Where had those tears come from? She hadn't wasted tears on her mother in years. 'And how can you leave your fourteen-year-old daughter behind?'

'She knew Melissa would look after you.'

'Melissa was only eighteen. She shouldn't have been

put in that position.' She inhaled deeply, trying to keep her composure, but the tears leaking from her eyes seemed to have a life of their own. 'She was as devastated as I was at what Mum was doing. She didn't want either of us to go. I can't remember whose idea it was for me to stay with her, whether it was hers or mine...'

Anna took a large drink of her wine and carefully wiped more tears away. She didn't want Stefano seeing her with smudged mascara, not tonight. 'I didn't want to go and I didn't want my mum to go either. I wanted her to stay and be my mum. I really thought if I refused to go that she would stay. Even when she bought me and Melissa the flat with Dad's insurance money and set up a monthly allowance for us I thought she'd stay. Right up until the moment her plane took off, I thought she would stay.'

The pain she'd experienced when she'd realised her mum had gone—had really gone—had been indescribable. It had been like having her heart stabbed with a thousand knives.

There was a long period of silence before a warm hand covered hers and sympathetic green eyes held her gaze.

'When did you last see her?' he asked.

'She came to England for my sixteenth birthday. That was her first and last visit. All she could talk about was how brilliant Australia was and how good Mick was to her. We had a massive argument. She called me and Melissa selfish bitches and said she was glad to be rid of us.' The words almost stuck in her throat. 'She flew back early.'

From the shock resonating in Stefano's eyes, it appeared this wasn't a part of the story she had shared before.

'Have you had any contact with her since then?'

She shook her head. 'She sends us cards and gifts for birthdays and Christmas, and she's written a couple of letters, but that's it.'

'What did the letters say?'

'I don't know. We burned them without reading them.'

The waiter returned to their table with their starters. Anna sniffed her *kung sadung nga*, deep-fried prawns in sesame batter and glazed in honey, and felt guilty for lowering the mood.

After all her good intentions she was in danger of ruining their last night here.

Before she could apologise, Stefano said thoughtfully, 'You've been coping with this for a long time. Do you think it's time for you to deal with it and talk to your mother and see if things can be mended?'

'You don't want to mend things with *your* family,' she said, stung.

'That's different. I will never forgive them for how they treated me. I will never forget. I don't want reconciliation. All I want is for them to see me rich and successful; everything that they are not. But my family is not yours. They never cared for me but your mother cared for you.'

'She left me,' Anna said, coldness creeping through her. 'How could she have cared for me?'

'You said yourself you were a proper family before your father died. She loved you then. I would guess she told herself she was doing the right thing.'

'I was a minor. I'd lost my dad, puberty had just struck...my head and emotions were all over the place. I needed her. Mel should have spent her uni years living

it up and behaving atrociously, not having to be guard-
ian to her bratty younger sister without any support from
the woman whose job it was to care for us. How can you
make excuses for that?'

'I'm not,' he said steadily, 'But Melissa clearly thinks
it's worth trying and you trust her.'

'But that's what I don't understand. What made Mel
change her mind? She hates Mum as much as I do. We've
always sworn we were better off without her.'

'You can't tell me you don't miss her.'

Suddenly terrified she would do more than leak tears,
Anna bit into one of her prawns and concentrated on not
crying.

Only when she was confident she could talk without
choking did she say, 'I'm sorry. I didn't want to ruin the
evening.'

'You haven't.' But his eyes had lost their sparkle.

'You're right that I've only been coping with it and
not dealing with it,' she admitted. 'You're the first person I've trusted since she got on that plane. Other than
Melissa.' Then, aware she was sinking the mood even
lower, forced a bright smile on her face. 'Don't let me
ruin the rest of the evening.'

'Anna…'

'No.' She put her hand on his and squeezed it. 'We
can talk about this when we get back to London and
reality, but our time here has been very special to me.
We're making good memories and I don't want my mum
spoiling them.'

A flicker of darkness crossed his features before he
gave the dazzling smile she loved so much and leaned
closer to her. 'We have a whole night to make even better memories.'

* * *

Night had fallen when they left the restaurant, lamps illuminating the streets, the sound of the Pacific clearer.

The longer the meal had gone on, the smaller the restaurant had seemed until it had shrunk to just the two of them. She hadn't seen anyone else. Her eyes had been only for Stefano. The restaurant had been busy but she couldn't describe a single diner or even remember the colour of their waiter's hair.

And Stefano's eyes had only ever been on her, seducing her, making her heart race so that she forgot she was eating possibly the best pad thai she'd ever tasted.

After the discussion about her mother he'd regaled her with gossip about the industry and his rivals, making her laugh aloud more than once.

But now, with the cool night air on her skin, her thoughts drifted back to her mother.

Her abandonment was a ten-year open wound.

Had her mum made a big deal during her one visit to England about how amazing Australia was in the hope her daughters would join her there? *Had* she missed them as much as they'd missed her?

She left you without a parent when you were only fourteen years old, Anna reminded herself.

It didn't change how much she missed her, even now. Stefano was right about *that*.

She'd been a loving mum, she remembered. Always busy, but always with a smile on her face. Quick to scold, but equally quick to forgive.

Her dad was gone from the earth. She carried an ache in her heart for him she knew would be there for the rest of her life, and accepted it. Welcomed it even, the pain a reminder of the father she had lost but would never forget. It was through no fault of his own that he'd missed the significant events in her life and she knew if he could be watching down on her then he would be.

Her mum was alive and well and missing all those moments by choice.

But she'd been there for Anna's sixteenth birthday.

Except she hadn't come back.

'You've gone quiet,' Stefano mused, his accented voice breaking through her reminiscences.

She squeezed her fingers tighter to his. 'Sorry.'

'Don't be. What are you thinking?'

'Nothing exciting,' she said, telling him the first untruth since she'd known him.

'I don't believe that what goes on in your brain is ever boring,' he teased.

'It's full of mundane trivia.'

'What is mundane?'

'Like boring.'

Without warning he dropped her hand and grabbed her shoulders, pulled her to him and kissed her fully and passionately.

And then just as quickly he broke away and took hold of her hand again. 'I bet your thoughts are not mundane now.'

He had that right.

By the time they returned to the beach house the only thing on her mind was making love to him.

When they stepped over the threshold, he gave her a long lingering kiss and said, 'Wait for me in the sunroom while I get us a drink.'

The lights of the sunroom were off, the only illumination coming from the night lights surrounding the swimming pool and bouncing through the wall of glass. It lent the room a romantic quality that perfectly suited her mood and her desire for one last perfect night here.

She looked out of the window and gazed at the dark ocean, only the distant flashes of foaming surf and the twinkling stars in the night sky differentiating one from the other.

Stefano came back into the room carrying two glasses of white wine. He joined her at the window, his arm brushing against her as he handed hers to her. 'Are your feet hurting yet?'

Startled at his question, Anna looked down at the fabulous shoes that, now she thought about it, were crippling her feet.

She must have been mad to wear such high heels on an evening that required walking. If she hadn't been so dazzled by their brilliance she would have worn flats and now her feet wouldn't ache so much.

'They're killing me.'

He tutted. 'I thought so. You always wear silly shoes.'

'They're not silly,' she said in mock outrage. 'I just happen to like nice shoes.'

'You have nice shoes that don't require you to cripple yourself wearing them.'

'If I wear heels it stops people tripping over me,' she said, deadpan.

He wiggled his left eyebrow in the way that always made her laugh, then took a large drink of his wine and put his glass on the low round table in the centre of the room. He took her hand and guided her to the rounded sofa that looked so much like a bed.

'Sit down,' he ordered.

'Bossy boots,' she said, deliberately taking a slow drink of her wine before obeying.

Stefano sat next to her, took hold of her ankles and put her feet on his lap.

'What are you doing?'

He unzipped the heel of her left shoe and gently tugged it off. 'Someone has to look after your feet if you won't,' he answered, a sparkle in his eyes. 'You are lucky you have married a man who gives fantastic foot massages.'

'And how do you know that?'

Her other shoe went the same way as the first. The relief to her poor feet was indescribable.

'*You* told me,' he said with a patient shake of his head, 'because you always insist on wearing silly shoes and then complain your feet hurt.'

The retort she had ready on her lips died away when he pressed his thumbs to the sole of her foot and slowly pushed up to her toes.

Stefano noted the way her eyes glazed as he began to massage her feet and experienced a thrill of satisfaction. Anna adored having her feet rubbed and right then he wanted to do nothing more than give her pleasure and wipe away the memories of her past he knew were suffusing her.

He would have given anything to stop her from talking earlier. He hadn't wanted to see her pain.

Dannazione, he shouldn't be aching to comfort her and wipe her demons away.

He could feel himself losing control of the situation and was determined to regain it.

'Put your head back and relax.'

A knowing smile playing on her lips, she placed her wine glass on the floor. Then she did as he'd suggested and lay with her head against the rounded softness of the sofa's back and her body in recline.

After massaging her left foot for a few minutes he switched to her right.

Anna sighed and finally closed her eyes. 'You really do give amazing foot massages.'

'I know.'

A snigger escaped her lips before she gave another deep sigh.

When he felt he'd worked enough on her foot, he moved his hand up to her ankle and then to her smooth calf, kneading the muscles with the pressure he knew she liked.

It occurred to him that he still knew far more about the responses of her body and what gave her pleasure than she did.

Up his hands went, over her knee, brushing the silk of her dress aside as he reached her thigh. This was where he had to be gentler, her inner thighs one of her most tender areas.

She kept perfectly still, only her deepening breaths indicating any response as his fingers inched ever upwards, his hand burrowing under her dress, deliberately keeping away from her most intimate area, teasing her, tormenting her.

Sliding his fingers back down her leg, he switched his attentions to her other leg and began the same sensuous trail.

Dio, but this was turning him on.

When he reached her thigh this time and kneaded his way to her hip, he hooked his finger into the side of her knickers.

Her breaths were now coming in ragged spurts, her cheeks flushed.

Taking hold of the elastic on her other hip, he gently

tugged her knickers down. When the soft dark hair between her legs was exposed, her eyes flew open.

There was such desire and trust in that stare. When
she looked at him like that all he could think was that he
wanted it to be like this between them always.

It was too late for thoughts like that. Too late to erase
the past. Too much had gone on between them but he
couldn't shake the thought that she'd said she trusted *him*
unaware that, come tomorrow, he planned to destroy her.

This would be his last gift to her.

Stefano threw her knickers onto the floor then placed
a hand on her ankle and gently pulled her legs apart. She
writhed beneath him and he pressed a hand to her belly
to steady her and placed a kiss on her inner thigh.

When he pressed his mouth into the heart of her she
gasped and jolted as if she'd had a volt of electricity shot
through her. A hand flailed out and touched his head.

He inhaled, breathing in her scent that he had never
tired of, *could* never tire of.

Taking greater care than he had ever done in his life,
checking his own ardour, which wanted nothing more
than to rip both their clothes off and take her without
ceremony, Stefano kissed and caressed the most intimate
part of her to gradually open her up to him.

The fingertips on his head moved imperceptibly in
tiny circular movements. Her breaths caught then deep-
ened and tiny moans escaped her lips. The fingers on his
scalp tightened and dug into him until finally, with the
breathiest of gasps, her back arched and she shuddered.

Only when he was certain her climax was over did he
haul himself up and put his hands either side of her head
to stare down at her.

Anna had faced down everything life had thrown at

her before, never flinching or hiding away. Over the past few days they had made love countless times, done everything possible, but this… This felt different. *She* felt different and opening her eyes to meet Stefano's gaze was one of the hardest things she'd ever done. She was afraid of what she would find there.

As she forced them open she knew the thing she most feared was not finding what she suddenly realised she so desperately wanted to see. Love.

She swallowed and met his gaze.

Her breath came unstuck again. If not love, there was tenderness in the dark, swirling green depths and it filled her chest so completely that she hooked her arms around his neck and pulled him down for a long kiss.

'You've got too many clothes on,' he said gruffly into her mouth, his hands sliding down to her waist.

'So have you.'

He made deft work of the belt. As soon as it was unclasped, her dress unwrapped itself, only one small button holding the last of the material together, which he undid with no effort before sliding an arm behind her back to unclasp her bra.

Gathering her to him, he pulled her up so he could slide the sleeves of her dress and bra down her arms, leaving her naked before him.

'*Dio*, you're beautiful,' he muttered.

'Your turn,' she whispered, lying back down. She stretched her arms above her head, luxuriating in his dilated gaze.

He removed his shirt, then got off the improbably large sofa only long enough to shed his trousers and underwear.

And then he was back on top of her, his mouth covering hers, and with one long thrust he was inside her.

He took her with a feverish passion, raising her thighs to drive into her as deeply as he could, deeper and deeper, faster and faster, their bodies fusing together to become one pulsating being.

Anna's climax bubbled back into life and when he came with a groan she followed within moments, biting into his shoulder and pressing herself as tightly as she could to him as the pleasure exploded out of her.

For a long, long time, the only sound to be heard was their ragged breathing and the thundering of their hearts.

It was the most blissful state.

Eventually Stefano shifted his weight off her and she twisted onto her side to rest her head on his chest.

She kissed the taut skin beneath her. 'I'm so glad I married you. I would do it again in a moment.'

His response was to tighten his hold on her and kiss the top of her head.

CHAPTER NINE

ANNA CARRIED HER BOWL of cereal to Stefano's study, eating as she went. For once he'd woken before her, waking her to make love before saying he had a conference call to take and work to catch up on. When she'd asked if there was anything she needed to be getting on with herself, he'd kissed her and reminded her that she was technically still off sick.

She hadn't protested. Five days of sex, sand and sea had left work far removed from her life. She'd left school at eighteen and had worked constantly since. There had been no grand plan, just a determination to work hard and be self-sufficient. She hadn't known how wonderful it could be to kick back and relax and to let the cares of the world pass her by and here, in this bustling beach paradise, she'd been able to do just that. In a few hours they'd be heading up Route 17 to San Francisco and their mini holiday in Santa Cruz would be over.

She found Stefano rummaging through a filing cabinet and talking to himself. It took her a moment to realise he was in fact having a video call with someone on his laptop.

He raised a hand and winked to acknowledge her and carried on with his conversation in rapid Italian with a woman Anna couldn't see from the angle of his laptop but whose voice replied in equally rapid Italian.

Perching herself on his desk, Anna ate her breakfast while the two chatted. Although she couldn't understand a word of what they were saying, judging by Stefano's tone this was no business talk.

By the time he'd finished the conversation, she'd finished her breakfast and put her bowl on his desk. 'Who was that?' she asked.

'My sister.' He came over to her, took her face in his hands and gave her a kiss.

She looped her arms around his neck. 'Is she okay?'

'She doesn't like her neighbours. She has three male students living in the flat above hers and they make too much noise at night. They ignore her complaints.'

'Is she not scary like you?'

'I don't scare people.'

'You revel in it.'

He grinned and kissed her again. 'Only people who deserve it. And I have never scared you.'

'I've never scared easily. So what are you going to do about her neighbours? Kneecap them?' she joked, then pressed her lips to his.

'I think a threatening letter will do as a start,' he said into her mouth.

She nipped his bottom lip. 'Very wise.'

Laughing, Stefano unlooped her arms from round his neck. 'I have a conference call to make. Give me an hour and I'll come back to bed before we leave.'

'You don't need me here for it?' She had never missed a conference call in all the time she'd worked for him...

But then she remembered she had a new role, one she

only had patches of memories of. She would have to get a handle on it from scratch.

She wouldn't worry about that until they were back in London, she decided, sliding off the desk.

'No underwear?' he said with a lascivious gleam.

She turned, giving a hint of her bare bottom beneath her skirt. 'I can sit on your lap.'

'You can sit on my lap any time you like. Just not when I'm taking a conference call.' He pushed her playfully. 'Now go.'

'Okay, okay, I know when I'm not wanted.'

He gave her a stern look that only made her laugh harder.

She sashayed deliberately to the door, a thought striking her as she made to leave. 'How do I get on with Christina?'

His brow furrowed.

'I ask because…well, I'm ashamed to say this but when I saw her getting out of your car last week…it felt like a knife in my heart.'

'What do you mean?'

'I assumed she was your latest girlfriend.' She must have seen the darkening in his eyes he wasn't quick enough to hide for she hastened to add, 'Don't forget, I had no idea we were married. I was used to your rolling conveyor belt of girlfriends, it was an easy mistake for me to make. I couldn't understand why it hurt to see you with what I thought was another lover.'

Stefano made sure not to show any reaction. Lying to Anna had been easy when she'd first had the amnesia diagnosed. Now, every untruth felt rancid in his guts. She didn't yet have the memories to know that she'd only met his sister the one time, when she'd walked into their London flat early that morning and found Christina wearing her robe. Anna not being able to speak Italian and Christina not speaking English had given them a language barrier that had allowed Anna to assume the worst.

It came to him how Christina had later described the scene.

'She went white,' his sister had said. 'I thought she was going to be sick. I tried to speak to her but she couldn't understand me; she kept shaking her head as if she'd seen something horrifying, and then she walked out.'

Did that really sound like the actions of a woman calculating how to turn a situation to her advantage?

Now he allowed himself to think about it with some distance from the aftermath, did it not sound like the actions of a woman who'd received a terrible shock?

'You and Christina have a language barrier,' he said steadily. That wasn't a lie.

She eyed him with the look of someone who knew something was being held back. Then she shrugged her shoulders. 'Maybe that's my cue to start learning Italian.'

He was saved from further talk of his sister by the tone on his laptop ringing out to notify him his conference call was about to start.

Anna shrugged again, a wry smile playing on her lips. 'And that's my cue to leave. Have fun.'

After she'd closed the door behind her, Stefano took the seat at his desk and accepted the call. While waiting for the others joining to connect, he rubbed his forehead.

The game he'd been playing, the revenge he'd been savouring…it sat like a bad taste on his tongue.

He'd learned more about his wife in the last week than he had in their entire marriage. Before she'd stormed into his boardroom and humiliated him that day he would never have dreamt she could be a gold-digger or that his trust in her could be unfounded. Every instinct in his guts and in his head were shouting at him that somehow, in some way, everything was wrong.

This was *Anna*. The woman he'd desired and admired from their very first meeting. The woman he'd trusted enough to pledge his life to...

His head began to burn and his guts twisted with something worse than nausea. With his revenge only hours away, he came to the realisation that he couldn't go through with it.

When his conference call was over he would call Miranda, the journalist he'd entrusted into his confidence, and tell her the embargoed press statement he'd given to her a week ago was to be scrapped and buried.

He'd get tonight's awards over with and then he would sit down with Anna and tell her the truth about everything.

The moment Anna walked into Stefano's apartment in San Francisco, more memories returned. Throughout their days in Santa Cruz, more and more had appeared. Her memory was like a giant jigsaw puzzle and what had started as a mammoth hunt for the pieces was now coming together rapidly.

'When did we get a new sofa?' she asked, surprised to find the plump white one replaced with chocolate-brown leather.

'You remember it?'

'It was my favourite thing here.' This apartment was furnished along the same lines as the London one, with everything designed to show off wealth and great taste.

She already missed their Santa Cruz beach house. For all its opulence, it had felt like a home.

He strode to the kitchen. 'It got damaged a few weeks ago. Tea?'

She followed him in. 'Looks like the concierge service has been in,' she said, noting the freshly cleaned scent of the place.

'I called them to get everything ready for us. We're eating at the hotel tonight but there's plenty of snack food if you're hungry...' Suddenly he turned to face her. 'Do you remember the concierge service here?'

She nodded and grinned. 'Like the one in London but with extra "have a nice day."'

'Your memories are coming back quickly now,' he observed.

'There are still holes but they're filling.'

At that, judging by the gleam in his eyes, his mind had taken an entirely different route. She was glad. Tension had been etched on his face since his conference call that not even a long bout of lovemaking before they'd left had been able to erase. When she'd asked what was troubling him, he'd said only that it was to do with work and that he'd tell her about it after the awards. With work still feeling a lifetime away, she didn't bother to pursue it.

'You have a filthy mind, Stefano Moretti.'

He pulled her into his arms and nipped at her earlobe. 'And you love it.'

Yes, she thought, yes, she did. She loved him.

But hadn't she already known she loved him? That tight, painful feeling that had been in her chest since she'd seen Christina follow him out of his car; that had been a symptom of it. It was liberating to finally acknowledge the truth to herself.

She loved him.

With only flat shoes on, her face was flat against his chest. She inhaled his scent greedily and sighed into him before tugging at his shirt to loosen it and slip a hand up it and onto his back.

The words rolled on her tongue, so close to being spoken aloud, but she held them back.

The last time she remembered saying those words had been to her father in the minutes before they'd turned his life support off.

Stefano gathered her hair and gently tugged her head back. 'You don't want tea?'

'I'm not thirsty.' She moved her hands to the front of his shirt and began undoing the buttons. She might not yet be able to say the words to him but she could show him. 'But I *am* hungry.'

As was always the case, Stefano was showered, shaved and ready a good hour before Anna, who'd had a beautician provided by the apartment's concierge service in to help her.

He pressed Miranda's name on his phone again and tapped his foot while waiting for it to connect.

He hadn't been able to get hold of her. He'd left her three messages and sent two emails. Anna had disappeared for a couple of hours' 'retail therapy' that afternoon and he'd tried Miranda again, even calling her newsroom.

Miranda Appleton was editor-in-chief of the US's best-selling celebrity magazine that had an accompanying website with the highest daily click rate of any media in the world. Miranda had her finger on the pulse of all celebrity news and in today's instant world a billionaire such as himself was considered a celebrity.

He'd chosen Miranda for his scoop because, for all her unscrupulous dealings, she was a woman of her word and he'd known she wouldn't break the embargo.

And now she had gone off-grid. No one knew where she was. No one could reach her.

His call went yet again to her voicemail.

'It's Stefano,' he hissed quietly down the line. 'Miranda, I need you to kill that story. I retract my statement. You cannot publish it. Call me back as soon as you can.'

Feeling sick to his stomach, he waited for Anna in the living room, sitting on the new sofa that had been delivered to replace the one he'd ruined when he'd made his first trip to San Francisco after she'd left him. He'd remembered making love to her on it and the rage that had ripped through him, which had caused him to rip up the one item of furniture she'd loved, pulling chunks out of it as *she* had ripped chunks out of *him*.

He'd been as out of control as he'd been before prison had cured him of his temper.

Jail itself hadn't been too bad but the six months he'd served behind bars had dragged interminably. He'd grown to hate the confinement, the suffocation that came from spending all day every day in an enclosed space surrounded by people there wasn't a hell's chance of escaping from. He understood why prisoners might turn to drugs, just to relieve themselves of the brain-numbing boredom. As he'd already been hooked on nicotine at the time he'd known better than to take that route himself. But, still, the days had been so *long*.

His temper had been the reason he'd been incarcerated. He'd walked out of those prison gates with a determination to never let it get the better of him again and until Anna had left him, he never had.

He took a deep breath then got up to pour himself a large measure of bourbon. He downed it in one, then poured another.

The doubts that had been amassing in his head since their arrival in California had grown. Yet he always came back to the fact of that damned letter from Anna's solicitor demanding a massive slice of his fortune. Whatever had been going on in her head at the time, that demand had come from *her*. He should not allow fantastic sex and the old sparring easiness they'd shared to overturn the facts of the situation because in that respect nothing had changed.

His plan had worked perfectly. He'd seduced her. She'd even said she would marry him again. That should fill him with satisfaction, not make him feel as if he'd been punched a dozen times in the gut.

Never in his life had he felt such indecision. Since his imprisonment he'd learned to keep a cool head, analyse the facts and then make up his mind. Once it was made up, nothing deterred him from his chosen path.

He shouldn't let the past week cloud his judgement or deter him from his path now.

But he'd learned more about his wife in the past week than he had in almost a year of marriage and all his instincts were telling him he couldn't go through with it.

Where on earth was Miranda? Had she got his messages?

They'd planned the timings down to the minute. His statement was due to go online halfway through the awards ceremony.

He heard soft footsteps approaching and composed himself.

Anna entered the living room serenely, like a goddess emerging from an oyster shell.

All the breath left his body.

She wore a floor-length fitted red lace dress that pooled at her feet like a mermaid's tail. The front plunged in a V showing the tiniest hint of creamy cleavage. Her bare arms glimmered. Her face was subtly made up except for the lips, which she'd painted the same shade as her dress, and her dark hair shone, blow-dried to fall thickly around her shoulders.

She spread her arms out and made a slow twirl. 'Well?'

He cleared his throat. 'I think I'm going to be the envy of every red-blooded male in attendance.'

Her eyes sparkled, joy resounding from them. 'I couldn't believe it when I found this dress in my dressing room. Did I buy it for tonight?'

'I assume so. I've only been on one shopping trip with you.'

She grinned. 'I remember that. Was it that bad for you?'

'I've had better times watching envelopes being stuffed.'

'I'd never been shopping with an unlimited credit card. Can you blame me for getting carried away?'

He shook his head, remembering the glee with which she'd attacked the shopping district he'd taken her to. He'd often given old girlfriends a credit card to buy themselves something for a night out and they'd always played a game; pretending to resist, pretending to want their independence and not wanting to take from him. Anna had made no such pretence. She'd snatched the card out of his hand—a card he'd given her to keep and not just for the one occasion—and raced to the shops like a roadrunner, virtually leaving a trail of dust in her wake. Her chutzpah had made him laugh.

And then he remembered a time before they'd married, when he'd caught her making calculations with a pen and paper. She'd been trying to work out her finances to see if she could afford to pay for her and her sister to go on a five-star spa weekend in Dublin for Melissa's birthday. He'd offered to pay and she'd dismissed it out of hand. She wouldn't even discuss it. He'd noticed in the weeks leading up to that particular spa break that she had brought her own lunch into the office rather than eating in the subsidised staff restaurant, and he'd admired that she was prepared to economise when necessary and forego little treats if it meant having a bigger treat at the end of it.

She'd often spent her money on her sister, he remembered, and for the first time wondered if it was her way of making up for Melissa giving up her freedom to raise her. For all Anna's current happiness, he knew Melissa wasn't far from her thoughts. He knew Melissa being in Australia with their mother had wounded her in ways he couldn't understand.

Anna had only been happy to spend his money *after* they'd married and that had only been to feed her addiction to clothes shopping. She'd cheekily described it as *the* perk of being his wife.

Miranda, check your damn messages.

'Where did you say the awards were being held?' Anna asked, rifling through her small red clutch bag.

'At the Grand Palace Hotel.'

Her hand stilled and she looked at him. 'The Grand Palace Hotel?'

'*Sì*. It's been held there for the past five years. What are you looking for?'

'Double-checking I've put my lipstick in,' she replied, but her eyes had glazed over, her words mechanical and said without any thought, her mind clearly somewhere else.

'What's wrong?'

After a moment she blinked and shook her head. Her mouth pulled into a smile but there was a brittleness to it. 'Nothing. Shall we go?'

Aware that to leave it much longer would make them late, he took her hand and together they left his apartment.

Only the cramping in his guts acted as a warning sign that something was very wrong.

CHAPTER TEN

ANNA'S NAILS, MANICURED FABULOUSLY by the beautician, dug into the palm of her hand. Stefano sat beside her in the back of the stretched Mercedes, filling the silence with talk of a new super-secure Cloud-based system his employees were developing. She made all the appropriate noises and asked all the obvious questions she would always ask but her thoughts were far away. A year ago away.

When he'd said they were going to the Grand Palace Hotel, she'd had an instant image flash in her head of being at that hotel with Stefano before, but just as the memory had crystallised another, equally vivid image had come to her of throwing a jug of water over him in his London boardroom, in front of the entire board of directors.

By the time they arrived at the hotel fifteen minutes after setting off, she wanted to tell the driver to turn round and take them back. She felt sick. Memories had come back to her—flooded back—and she wanted to sit somewhere on her own and make sense of them all.

Because none of it made sense. She'd already remembered arguments between them and had accepted them without dissection. She would have been more surprised if they hadn't argued. She remembered missing him when he went away on business without her and, shaming as it was, remembered the fears and insecurities that had crept up on her.

What she hadn't remembered until only a few minutes ago, and which Stefano hadn't bothered to mention, was that she'd left him. More than that, she'd confronted him in his boardroom and lost total control of herself in front of everyone. What she still couldn't remember was why or what the aftermath had been.

She had almost the entire picture there before her but the biggest, most significant pieces were still missing. Her painfully thudding heart told her that she didn't want to remember.

The car door was opened and before either of them had moved from their seats, lights flashed around them.

The Tech Industry Awards, if one was to go by its name, promised nothing more than a bunch of eggheads crowded together in a room congratulating each other on their supreme eggheadedness. The truth was that these awards were prestigious and glamorous enough to rival the ceremony for any national film or music award. These were the awards the big players wanted and paid a fortune to sponsor. It was estimated the collective worth of the attendees this evening would make up the largest concentration of money in the world, and the press was out in force to cover it.

Above them, thick dark clouds had gathered. Anna gave an involuntary shiver. A storm was on its way and her foreboding only grew.

She made sure to keep her face inscrutable as she climbed out and took Stefano's hand. Ignoring the shouts from reporters throwing inane questions at them—she distinguished at least three asking 'who' she was wear-ing—they went through the cordon opened for them. Waving at the thick crowd of spectators, they walked up the red carpet where only a select few journalists were allowed to stand.

As they passed one reporter doing a piece for camera, she caught some of what was being said.

'Rumours of the Moretti marriage being over have been scotched by the couple's first public appearance in six weeks.'

And then the reporter swung round and thrust the microphone in Stefano's face.

'If you could choose one award to win tonight, which would it be?'

'I couldn't choose just one,' Stefano answered with the easy smile that made millions of women around the world long to bed him. 'But whether we win anything tonight or not makes no matter. Moretti's is the leading software manufacturer and app developer in the world, and the technology my dedicated staff are developing will change the face of the world as we know it.'

'Fabulous!' The reporter gave the vacuous grin that meant she hadn't listened to a word of his answer and im-mediately turned her microphone to Anna. 'What do you have to say, Anna, about the reports on your marriage?'

Anna responded with an identical vacuous smile. 'What reports are you referring to?'

The reporter's composure wavered for only a second. 'The rumours that you had separated. Are we to believe that you two are still together?'

Stefano put his arm around her waist and opened his mouth to speak, but Anna couldn't bear to hear another of his lies.

She smiled and made sure to inject sweetness in her voice. 'I think my presence here with my husband can speak for itself. Enjoy your evening.'

And with a gracious nod and another wave to the crowd, Anna and Stefano were taken inside by a couple of burly bouncers.

His arm stayed around her waist in that protective fashion she'd always so adored. Outwardly he appeared completely unfazed by the reporter's remarks. He'd buttered her up well for it, she thought cynically. Hadn't he remarked when she'd been in the hospital that the press were always speculating on the state of their marriage?

If only she could remember those last pieces of the scene, she would know what had come after she'd drenched him in water.

Knowing Stefano as well as she did, she didn't think it was something he would have easily forgiven her for.

If only she knew what had compelled her to do it in the first place...

Now was not the time to try and work it all out, not in a reception hall filled with industry bigwigs all wanting to shake hands, exchange stories and assert individual dominance. There was a convivial atmosphere, however, as rivalries were set aside for the night, at least superficially.

The Moretti table was situated directly before the main stage and thus in the glare of the majority of the video cameras. Anna kept her head held high as they joined the executives and company nominees who'd been invited to join them on this prestigious night, pretending not to see the curious glances being flashed her way.

Only one member of the UK board was in attendance, the rest from Sweden, Japan and America. She knew with one look that they all knew exactly what had happened in that boardroom. And they knew she had received her P45 for gross misconduct the very next day and had had no contact with any member of staff or with her husband...

Until the morning she'd woken with a bang on her head and her memories wiped.

And now, she remembered...

It explained everything. All the stares she'd received, Chloe's appropriation of her desk, Stefano's anger...

She remembered everything.

Everything.

Oh, how she wished she hadn't. Ignorance had been more than bliss; it had been an escape from the unbearable agony that had become her life.

Stefano put his hand on hers. Her veins turned to ice and she fought not to snatch it away. He whispered something in her ear and she fought not to flinch.

She made sure to keep a smile on her face and play the role of the happy wife. It was the greatest role she'd ever had to play.

When Moretti's was given its third award of the night and Stefano took to the stage with the innovative hipster who'd been the brains behind it, she clapped as hard as everyone else.

Her pride would not allow her to show publicly that her heart had been irreversibly broken.

But she couldn't keep it together for ever.

Not long after the halfway point of the evening she rose from the table.

Stefano grabbed her wrist. 'Where are you going?'

'To the Ladies'.'

'Can't you wait?' His nostrils were flared, his jaw clenched.

'*What?*' She snatched her hand away. 'Don't be ridiculous.'

As she hurried her way through the tables she became aware that shocked faces were staring at her. Voices at every table she approached dropped to a hushed whisper and there was a furious tapping of phone screens accompanied by more shocked faces.

Fortunately the ladies' room was empty. She wished there were a window she could crawl out of but if all she could have was a few moments to compose herself then she would take that.

Sucking in some deep breaths, she pressed powder to her white cheeks and fixed her eyeliner and lipstick, then took some more deep breaths for luck and left her brief sanctuary.

The stares and whispers were even more pronounced now. There was still a handful of awards left to be given but Stefano had risen from their table and was taking great strides towards her.

'We need to go,' he said, grabbing her hand and practically dragging her to the exit.

'It's not finished yet.' As much as she longed to escape the stares, protocol dictated that everyone should stay to the bitter end.

He didn't answer or slow his pace. If anything he moved faster.

If he could get her out of the hotel and into his car before the press noticed them, Stefano knew he had a chance. A chance to explain himself before Anna learned of the bomb he'd detonated.

The weather had taken a turn for the worse since their arrival. Thick droplets of rain were falling and the breeze had picked up.

They almost made their escape. The press were too busy huddled together in little clusters, staring at their phones, chattering frenziedly among themselves, to notice the couple slipping out half an hour early or the gathering storm around them.

But then a driver got out of a yellow cab and called out loudly, 'Anna Moretti?' and with a violent curse, Stefano knew he was too late.

He'd forgotten his instruction that Miranda book a cab for Anna and to make sure the driver arrived early with a picture of the passenger he was to collect. Stefano had planned to put her in it as his final flourish, to shut the door for her and never see her again.

His plan had worked perfectly.

Success had never tasted so bitter.

At the mention of Anna's name the press sprang into action.

Pounding feet rushed towards them, a babble of shouted words pouring out so thick and fast they should be incomprehensible. But judging by the pallor of Anna's face and the tiny stumble she made, she had heard them clearly enough.

His own driver pulled up. Stefano opened the back door himself and bundled Anna's rigid body inside.

It was only as he slammed the door behind them that he caught a glimpse of Miranda Appleton standing like a vulture next to her magazine's photographer, a smirk on her ugly, rancid face.

Anna sat like a mannequin pressed against the far door. She didn't look at him. She hardly seemed to be breathing.

The rain had turned into a deluge and the driver slowed to a crawl. With the silence stretching between them and an air of darkness swirling, it was a relief when they eventually came to a stop at the front of the apartment building. A crackle of lightning rent the sky, illuminating everything for a few brief seconds that were still long enough for him to see the shock carved on her frozen face.

She didn't notice they'd come to a stop.

'Anna,' he said tentatively. 'We're home.'

Still she sat there, immobile.

Only when he leaned over to take her hand—*Dio*, it was icy to the touch—did she show any animation.

Slowly her head turned to face him. 'Don't touch me.'

Then, with no care for any passing cars, she opened her door and stepped out into the deluge.

Stefano jolted after her and breathed a tiny sigh of relief that the road was empty of traffic.

Maybe it was the lashing rain that forced her hand but she walked sharply into his apartment building. She bypassed the elevator to take the stairs, her heels clip-clopping without pause all the way to the eighteenth floor.

There was no sign of her exertion when she shrank away from him as he punched in the entry code to their apartment.

She headed straight to their bar, snatched up the nearest bottle and took a huge gulp from it. Then she took another gulp, wiped her mouth with the back of her hand and put the lid back on.

Only then did she meet his eye.

She stared at him for an age before her face contorted into something unrecognisable and she smashed the bottle down on the bar with all her strength.

'Bastard!' she screamed as the bottle exploded around her, then reached for a bottle of brandy and smashed that

too. The single malt went next, all accompanied by a hail of curses and profanities that seemed to be wrenched from her very soul.

The bourbon would have gone the same way had Stefano not sprung into motion—the destruction had happened within seconds—and wrapped his arms around her, trapping her back against his chest.

'Anna, stop,' he commanded loudly. 'You're going to hurt yourself.'

She thrashed wildly in his hold, kicking her legs backwards and forwards, catching his shin with the heel of her shoe, all the while screaming curses at him.

He winced at the lancing pain but didn't let her go.

In a way, the pain was welcome. He deserved it.

She caught his shin again and he gritted his teeth. 'Please, stop fighting me. I know you want to hurt me. I *know*. And I deserve it. Hit me, kick me, bite me, do whatever you want but please, *bellissima*, don't hurt yourself. There's glass everywhere.'

As if she could hurt herself after what he'd done to her. In the state she was in, he doubted she would feel any pain.

His words must have penetrated for gradually the fight went out of her and she went limp in his arms.

Cautiously he released his hold and braced himself for her to take him at his word and attack him.

Instead, she staggered to the centre of the living room and flopped to the floor. The mermaid tail of her dress made a perfect semi-circle around her. Her chest rose heavily and she lifted her head to stare at him. Misery and contempt pierced him.

Without saying a word, she removed each sparkling shoe in turn. There was a moment when he thought she was going to throw them at him but, after a small hesitation, she flung them to her side.

When she finally spoke there was a metallic edge to her tone that made his veins run cold.

'Did you enjoy your revenge?'

'I tried to stop it.' He knew it was a pathetic thing to say even before her face twisted.

He dragged a hand through his hair and took a deep breath before reaching carefully through the debris of glass for the saved bottle of bourbon.

'You couldn't have tried very hard.' She laughed, a robotic sound that made him flinch. 'I think your revenge worked. The ruthless Stefano Moretti shows the world that you mess with him at your peril, even if you're his wife. My humiliation will make front page news everywhere.'

He unscrewed the bottle and put it to his lips. The liquid burned his throat.

'It was too late to stop it. Miranda must have known I'd change my mind. She made it impossible for me to contact her.'

'Miranda Appleton? That witch?'

He nodded and drank some more.

'You're blaming *her*?'

'No. The only one to blame for tonight is me. I set it up.' After everything that had been said and done between them, the only thing they were left with was the truth. 'I called her last week, the day after I brought you home from hospital, and gave her a statement. I put an embargo on it that was to be lifted at nine thirty this evening.'

'And what did your statement say?' Though she was outwardly calmer, he could see she was clinging to her control by a whisker.

'That the rumours about our marriage were true and that I would be issuing you with divorce papers tomorrow morning.'

'Happy anniversary to me.'

'At the time I thought it fitting.'

'And all the times you made love to me? Treated me like a princess? Cared for me? Where did that all fit in? I suppose that was to humiliate me privately as well as publicly so that every time I thought of us together in Santa Cruz, the city I love, I would be reminded that I'd been a fool to think I could take you on and win?'

She knew him too well. Better than he knew himself.

Shame rolled through him like a dark cloud. He jerked a nod. There was nothing he could say to defend himself. He didn't want to even try.

'The cab? Where was that going to take me?' she asked.

'Out of my life.'

She laughed again. He had never heard such a pitiful sound.

'So, if I'm to believe you'd changed your mind—and in fairness I can see you got cold feet about the cab side of it, so let's give you the benefit of the doubt about that—what brought the change of heart about? You've played me like a violin all week to reach this point so why back out at the last minute?'

'I've been having doubts.'

She trembled but her voice remained steady. 'Doubts? That's a good one. Doubts about what?'

'About whether you really had set out to frame me for adultery and fleece me for as much money as you could get all along.'

Pain lashed her features. 'That's what you believed?'

He gripped the bottle tightly. He'd been so caught up with all that had just happened that he'd lost sight of what had driven him to these actions in the first place.

He'd done wrong—he knew that—but she had too.

'You're the one who found a strange woman in our apartment and immediately decided I was having an affair.'

She shook her head with incredulity. 'If you'd come back early from a trip abroad and found a strange semi-naked man in the apartment, what would you have thought?'

Stefano's heart was thumping violently against his ribs. 'I do not say I wouldn't have been a little suspicious but I wouldn't have made assumptions as you did.'

No, if he'd found a strange man in his apartment wearing his robe, his fist would probably have connected with the man's face before he'd had time to think.

'I would have asked you to explain,' he continued, pushing the thought away. 'I would have listened to your answer. You didn't ask for my side. *You* decided the facts to suit yourself. You swore at me and threw water over me in front of my most senior members of staff. You humiliated me.'

'You were ignoring me.'

'When?'

'That night. I called. It went to voicemail…'

'My sister who I didn't know existed had suddenly appeared in my life,' he interrupted. 'I had just been told the father I thought had died when I was a child had been alive all these years and had a new family but that there was no chance of me meeting him because he had died a few weeks before. Forgive me if I was too busy trying to make sense of my life to answer my phone.'

He hadn't even noticed it ring. Christina had sent a courier to his apartment with a letter and some photos—photos of *him* as a child—ending her note with a number for him to call.

She'd been waiting outside the apartment building.

'Too busy to answer the phone for your *wife*? Too busy to call when I left a message *and* texted you asking you to call me?'

'I didn't get the messages until four in the morning when it was too late to call you back, but I did text you. I told you I would call you later in the day, which I would have done after the meeting you interrupted, but you jumped to the conclusion that I was with another woman. You stormed into my boardroom and accused me of having an affair in front of my most senior members of staff. You threw water over me.' As the humiliation flooded back over him, his temper rose. 'You broke your word. You said you would trust me. You lied to me!'

Anna stared at him for the longest time, her lips parted but with no sound coming out. But then the colour rushed back across her cheeks and she got to her knees to thump the floor.

'You selfish, selfish *bastard*. Twisting this all round to hide what you've done. I've made mistakes and done things I'm ashamed of but you took advantage of my amnesia just so you could have your revenge. You let me think I still worked for you! No wonder you didn't want me calling Melissa—that wasn't for my sake, it was to protect your lie! You've been lying to me for over a week!'

'You hit me with a demand for a hundred million pounds!' he shot back. 'You knew I wouldn't take that lying down.'

'Of course I knew that! Why do you think I issued it?'

'You *wanted* me to react?'

'I wanted you to speak to me and I was crazy enough
to think that demanding a hundred million and a load of
your assets would force you to communicate. You'd cut
me off. You fired me and blocked my number. You served
me with formal separation papers. You changed the se-
curity number for the apartment so I couldn't get in. It
was like I'd never existed for you. I wanted to hurt you
as much as you were hurting me. I knew the only way I'd
be able to get your attention was by hitting you where I
knew it would hurt the most—your wallet.'

'You walked out on *me*,' he reminded her harshly. 'Did
you think I would beg you to come back?'

'I came back the next day and couldn't get into the
apartment. You didn't even give me twenty-four hours
before locking me out.'

The cold mist in his head had thickened, nausea roil-
ing in his guts as he thought of his own contribution to
the mess that was the end of their marriage. He *had* cut
her off. His pride and ego had been dented so greatly that
he'd struck back before she could do any more damage.

'Why did you want to get my attention so badly?'

'Because I needed you and because, despite everything, I couldn't accept we were over.' She pinched the
bridge of her nose and held out her other hand for the
bottle. He took a nip himself before passing it to her.

She took a long slug.

'Don't you think you've had enough?'

Her hair swished as she shook her head. 'Nowhere
near enough.'

The trembling anguish in her voice sent a fresh roll
of dread through him.

Her hands were shaking so much the bottle slipped

from her hand and onto her lap, then rolled onto the floor.

In silence they watched the transparent fiery liquid spill onto the dark carpet.

'Anna,' he said quietly, 'why did you say you needed me?'

Her face rose to meet his gaze. Her eyes were stark, her bottom lip trembling.

All these weeks he'd been determined to think the worst. Anna had made assumptions but he had too. He could admit that.

She swallowed a number of times before saying in a voice so small he had to strain to hear, 'I lost our baby.'

'What...?' The question died on his lips as the cold mist in his head froze to ice.

The devastation on her face was so complete that he knew with gut-wrenching certainty that he hadn't mis-heard her.

He could no longer speak. His tongue felt alien in his mouth.

He gazed at his wife's white face and huge pain-filled eyes and the room began to spin around them. His heart roaring in his ears, he reached out blindly for her but then his knees buckled beneath him and he groped the arm of the nearest chair before they gave way completely.

Dio, what had he done?

CHAPTER ELEVEN

ANNA, HER STOMACH CHURNING, bile rising inside her, clenched her hand into a fist and shoved it against her mouth to stop herself from screaming.

How she'd prevented the screams from ripping out of her when it had all come back to her that evening she didn't know, could only guess it had been iron determination not to let the liar she'd married see her misery or the avid curious faces of their peers that had made her succeed. But now the words were out and there was no putting them back and it hit her like a tsunami that had been gathering into a peak and now came crashing down on her.

That last piece of her memory had come when she'd glanced at the menu in the hotel and read that their first course was smoked duck.

She'd been eating smoked duck in their Parisian hotel when she'd confessed to Melissa that her period was three days late.

She'd never seen Stefano lost for words before, never seen him be anything but arrogantly self-possessed. Seeing the colour drain from his horror-struck face sliced through the protective shield she'd been clinging to and her whole frame collapsed.

She fell onto her side and brought her knees up to her chin, wrapping her arms around them, and wept as she hadn't done since she was fourteen years old and she'd woken to the realisation that she would never see her father again.

The pain was unbearable, carving through her like a white-hot knife.

Through the sobs racking her body, she was aware of movement. Stefano had shifted to sit beside her on the floor.

It only made her sob harder. It was as if she were purging herself of all the pain in one huge tidal wave of grief. The loss of her father, her mother's desertion, her sister's betrayal and, fresher and more acute than all this, the loss of the man she loved and the child she'd so badly wanted.

That was something else her amnesia had anaesthetised her against: her increasingly desperate need for a child. Stefano's child. She'd sensed her marriage fragmenting around her and had tried to push the need aside, knowing theirs wasn't the stable marriage one should bring a child into. It hadn't stopped her craving one and when she'd discovered she was pregnant her joy had been so pure and true that for a few magical hours she'd allowed herself to believe that everything would work out between them and that Stefano would stop pushing her away and let her into his heart.

Now, with her memories acutely fresh, she had to accept what she'd been unable to accept in the month before she'd hit her head and slipped into blissful ignorance: that their relationship was over and all her dreams were dead.

It was a long time before the tears stopped flowing and her shuddering frame stilled enough for her to think clearly again. Her chest and throat sore, she dried her eyes with the hem of her dress and hauled herself into a sitting position with her legs crossed as she'd sat when she had been a child.

Stefano, who hadn't said a word, stretched his legs out beside her and gave a long sigh. 'You were pregnant?' he asked in a tone of voice she'd never heard before. He sounded...defeated.

She gulped for air, wishing with all her might that she could lapse back into ignorant bliss. 'Do you remember I switched the contraceptive injection I was using?'

He nodded jerkily.

'I forgot it was an eight-week course and not a twelve-week like the old one.' She sucked in more air, remembering how all over the place she'd been emotionally at that time, how her fears about her marriage had come to cloud everything. 'When I told Melissa I was three days late she couldn't believe I hadn't done a pregnancy test. She dragged me around Paris looking for a chemist so we could buy one.' She almost smiled at the memory. It was pretty much the first time in a long while that she had been happy and the last time she and Melissa had been comfortable with each other. 'I didn't think I was. I thought it was the kind of thing women knew instinctively.'

'But you were?'

She nodded and swallowed back the choking feeling in her throat. 'I was going to wait until the morning before I did the test but I couldn't resist doing it when we got back to the hotel. I was so distrustful of the result that I dragged Melissa back out to get another one and that came out positive too. That's why I called you. I was so happy I couldn't wait to tell you.' She cast him a rueful stare. 'And I was feeling a bit guilty for not taking the test with you.'

He raised a weary shoulder. 'It doesn't matter. You do everything with your sister. I'm used to it.'

'You think that but Melissa didn't see it that way,' she whispered. 'We *used* to do everything together, until I married you. I didn't realise how lonely she was without me. After I left that message for you to call me back she sat me down and told me she was going to Australia.'

Stefano whistled quietly.

'She'd been planning it for months. She'd been secretly speaking to Mum and arranging it all. She'd booked her flights, booked the time off work... All she'd been waiting for was the right time to tell me. She picked her moment perfectly, when I was on top of the world with news of the pregnancy to dull the impact of it.'

'And did it?'

'Nope.' She wiped away a tear. 'We had a huge fight. We said some *horrible* things to each other. She called me a selfish bitch and she was right—I was. It was all about *me* and how I felt. See? Selfish. I left her in the hotel and went to the airport and stayed there until I could get a flight back to London in the morning. I didn't sleep at all. I kept hugging my phone waiting for you to call me back. I was desperate to speak to you. I can't describe how I felt—on the one hand thrilled and elated that we were going to be parents, a little scared of how you'd react, and devastated at what I perceived as Melissa's betrayal.'

'Why were you scared of my reaction?' he asked hollowly.

She wiped away fresh tears, struggling to keep her

voice audible. 'You'd become so distant. I knew you were angry that I suspected there were other women but I *didn't* believe it. I *did* believe you but when you gave me that promotion and started travelling abroad without me...I thought you were bored of me.'

Stefano's voice cracked as he said, 'I promoted you because you were the best person for the job and I knew I could travel abroad leaving my company in the best hands.'

Promoting Anna had been a business decision. Anyone lucky enough to employ her would have done the same. And the time apart had done them good. Had done *him* good. Being together day and night hadn't been healthy. He'd expected their marriage to be eventful and fun. He hadn't expected to want to strip the skin from Anna's body to discover the secrets of her heart.

That had been dangerous. Unhealthy.

He'd thought some distance was necessary. He hadn't realised it would feed into her insecurities.

'I became paranoid. I couldn't sleep for thinking of all the women who would be flaunting themselves before you, lining themselves up to replace me.' Her red eyes were huge on his. 'I was terrified one of them would catch your eye and then the press published those pictures of you. I knew you were telling me the truth but by then I thought it was only a matter of when. I would wake every day wondering if it would be our last, always thinking, *Is this the day he meets someone else? Is this the day he tells me we're over?*'

'Anna, I made a promise to be faithful to you.'

'No, you promised to tell me if you met someone you wanted to sleep with so I could walk away with my dignity intact.'

'I kept that promise. I never cheated on you. I never wanted anyone else. I never gave you reason to doubt me.'

'Stefano, our marriage was based on two things. Sex and work. When you started pulling away from me and leaving me behind it was like you didn't need me any more. I knew you would never love me but I didn't think it mattered. I thought it was a good thing, better than having someone say they would love me for ever and then cheat and break my heart.' She shrugged and gave a choking laugh, then put her hand under her nose and closed her eyes. 'Oh, the lies we tell ourselves,' she whispered. 'I was already in love with you when we married but in total denial about it. What I really wanted was for you to tell me you didn't need to make that promise. I wanted you to say there would never be anyone else for you but me.'

The spinning in the room had turned into a whirlpool.

How could he have been so blind? So busy running from his own feelings that he'd dismissed Anna's fears thinking his word alone should be good enough for her.

He was feeling now. Feeling more than he had ever wanted, feelings he'd spent his life escaping from.

'And then you found Christina in the apartment,' he stated quietly.

She lifted her knees to wrap her arms around them and rocked forward. 'I lost my mind. Seeing a beautiful woman in our apartment dressed in my robe; it was my worst nightmare come to life. I wanted to hurt you. I was out of my mind. Truly, I wasn't thinking straight. What I did in your boardroom... I am so ashamed. I don't blame you for cutting me off as you did. I brought it on myself.'

Every word that Anna said plunged like a knife into Stefano's heart. How could she blame herself? This was all on him. If he hadn't been so full of outraged wounded pride he would have seen something had been seriously wrong with his wife.

But he hadn't thought of her. He'd thought of only himself.

Eventually he was able to drag out of his frozen throat the question he most feared hearing the answer to. 'What happened to the baby?'

'I lost it two days later.' A huge shudder ran through her and she buried her face in her knees, fresh sobs pouring out of her.

Feeling as if he'd been kicked in the stomach, Stefano pulled her to him. This time he allowed his instincts to take over, wrapping his arms tightly around her, pressing his mouth into her hair, wishing he knew the words that would make everything better and stop the cold agony he knew was consuming them both.

She clutched at his jacket, her tears soaking into his shirt. 'It was the only thing keeping me going. I know it must sound stupid but I'd pictured our baby. I'd planned its whole life out in my head...'

'It doesn't sound stupid at all,' he cut in. In his mind's eye he could picture their baby too...

Fresh bile rose swiftly inside him and grabbed at his throat, making his head spin.

'Where were you when you...?' He couldn't bring himself to say it.

'In my hotel room.' She took a gulp of air. 'I'd checked into a hotel because I couldn't face Melissa after our row and you wouldn't let me anywhere near you.'

'You were alone?'

She nodded into his chest. 'So, selfish creature that I am, I went back to my sister.'

'You are *not* selfish,' he stated fiercely.

Anna had had to go through that trauma on her own? The only selfish one here had been him.

'Aren't I? I hated the thought of her seeing our mum.'

'No,' he contradicted, 'you were scared you would lose her too. You lost both your parents when you were at an age when you needed them most. Your father, rest his soul, did not leave by choice but your mother did. Is no wonder you find it hard to trust people—the woman who should have been there for you left you behind.'

And if he'd ever allowed Anna to open up to him during their marriage instead of avoiding any kind of intimate talk he would have known how shattered her mother's emigration had left her. He would have known just how vulnerable she was and would have made that damned call to her instead of telling himself she would be fast asleep and wouldn't mind waiting.

You did know she'd mind but you were running scared. Anna got too close, didn't she? You were waiting for an excuse to push her away before she rejected you like everyone else you ever knew did.

She hadn't been asleep. She'd been in an airport waiting to return home to him with the best news of their lives and some shattering news of her own. She'd needed him.

He squeezed her even tighter to him. 'Melissa looked after you?'

'Melissa always looks after me.' Anna tilted her head to look at him. 'She's always been my lifeline, and you're right, I was scared I'd lose her. We muddled along as well as we could but it was hard. We'd both said things we couldn't take back. When she left for Australia it was without my blessing. She even left me a note asking for my forgiveness when it should have been me down on my knees begging for hers.'

'Anna...'

'No, please don't make excuses for me. I'm not fourteen any more. I've always known how much Melissa missed our mum but ignored it under my own self-righteousness.'

'Or did you ignore it because it meant you would have to confront how much you missed your mum too?'

'Don't say that,' she protested.

'You must have missed her. I always missed my mother and I never even knew her.'

'Did you?'

She sounded so surprised that he couldn't help but give a grimace of a smile. 'All my life. And I missed my father. I look now on all the years we missed out on when I could have known him and I think what a waste those years were.'

'But do you regret cutting the rest of your family out of your life?'

'Not at all. I will never have them in my life again but my situation with them is different from yours. I never loved them and they never loved me.'

Since his *nonno* had died, Anna was the only person who had loved him. Lots of women had claimed to love him but he'd always known their words to be a pack of lies. Anna was...

She was the only one.

'You still think I should see my mother?'

'You will never find peace until you do, that much I do know. Speak to her. Hear her side. Admit to yourself that you need her in your life. See if you can build a re-lationship.'

She fell silent.

'I can come with you.'

'Where?'

'To see your mother. I can come as support.'

Her laugh sounded genuine but as she disentangled herself from his hold he saw fresh tears were streaming down her face.

'I needed your support five weeks ago.' She shook her head and wiped the tears away then straightened.

'Let me give it to you now,' he urged. 'I wasn't there for you...'

'No, you weren't.' Her shining eyes bored into his. 'And I don't blame you. I understand what a shock it must have been for you having your sister turn up out of the blue and learning about your father.'

'I should never have cut you off.'

'No, you shouldn't, but I knew the type of man you were when I married you. I knew you didn't do forgive-ness. One strike and the person's out—humiliating you was my strike and I accept that...'

'No, don't accept it. I was a *fool* to behave like that.' A fool and a cruel, selfish bastard. 'If I'd any idea what you were going through I would never have...'

'It doesn't matter!' She took a deep breath and got un-steadily to her feet. 'None of it matters any more, don't you see that? Our marriage is over and it's time I learned to stand on my own two feet.'

The freezing fog in his brain thickened, making his ears ring. 'It doesn't have to be over. We can start again.'

'It does.' She folded her arms across her chest. There was something in her stance that made her appear taller.

'We could forgive each other everything that happened, draw a line in the sand and start again, but I'll never forgive you for what you did to get your revenge.' She shrugged her shoulders but the whiteness of her face belied the nonchalance she was trying to portray. 'That was despicable and I hate you for it.'

On legs that were surprisingly weak, he got up to stand before her. Something was scratching at him, clawing at his chest, making it painful to breathe. 'You said that you loved me.'

'And I did love you. With all my heart. All through my amnesia I kept thinking you were holding back from telling me you loved me to keep the pressure off my recovery but the truth was you never loved me, did you?'

The pain in his chest increased. He couldn't form any words. Not one.

'You killed my love and all my trust in you,' she spat. 'If I ever marry again it will be to someone who wants more than just my body and my business brain.' Her voice caught but when she continued her tone didn't falter. 'It will be with someone who can love me too and trust me with their heart. I have to hope for that.'

And with that she turned her back on him, picked up her clutch bag from the table and headed for the front door.

'Where are you going?' Things were moving too quickly. She couldn't just *leave* like this. 'Look at the weather out there.'

The rain was lashing so hard it fell like hail against the windows.

She didn't turn around. 'I'm going to check into a hotel and in the morning I'm going to go home. *My* home. Mine and Melissa's flat. After that, all I know for certain is that I have to stop relying on other people to hold me up and learn to hold myself up. If Melissa stays in Australia then I will give her my blessing.' Then she did turn and gave the smallest, saddest of smiles. 'Maybe I will fly out there too. I don't know.'

There was nothing left to say. He could see it in her eyes. Anna was going to walk out of the door and this time it would be for good.

She didn't say goodbye.

She closed the door with the softest of clicks but the sound echoed like a ricocheting bullet.

Stefano stood on the same spot for an age, too numb and dazed about everything that had just happened to take it all in. A part of him expected—hoped—that the door would swing back open and she'd walk back in and tell him she'd changed her mind.

It didn't happen.

Her discarded shoes lay on their sides where she'd thrown them. Her feet were bare...

His legs suddenly propelled themselves to the window that overlooked the street below. He pushed it open and stuck his head out, uncaring that the storm soaked him in seconds and blinded his eyes.

Through the sheet of water running over his face he caught a glimpse of a red dress disappearing into a cab. Seconds later the cab pulled away from the kerb and soon he lost sight of it.

Anna had gone.

A week later Stefano strolled through the entrance foyer of his London apartment building. The two receptionists on duty greeted him warmly but with the same subtle wariness he'd been receiving at work that had become more marked since his return from San Francisco. He was used to fear but this felt different. Now people treated him as they would when confronted with a dangerous dog they didn't want to provoke.

Anna had treated him like that before she'd collapsed at his feet with her concussion.

He blinked her image from his mind.

It mattered nothing to him how his staff behaved towards him. He preferred everyone to keep their distance. He didn't need their chatter. If someone wanted to speak to him, he was all for getting to the point, cut the chit-chat and get on. Small talk was discouraged.

Anna had taught him the term 'cut the chit-chat'. It had made a sharp but smooth sound in his mouth that amused him. *Had* amused him. It had been a long time since he'd found anything funny.

He took the bundle of letters one of the receptionists held out for him with a nod and was about to continue to the elevator when he remembered Anna's not so subtle way of pulling him up on his manners those two and a half years ago.

With two short sarcastic words, *you're welcome*, she'd reminded him that being Europe's top technology magnate didn't stop you or the others around you being human and that humans needed to feel appreciated.

He paused, looked the receptionist in the eyes and said, 'Thank you,' then wished them both a good evening and carried on up to his apartment.

Only after he'd dumped his briefcase and poured himself a bourbon did he sit on the sofa and go through his mail.

He put his thumb and middle finger to the bridge of

his nose and squeezed to keep himself alert but, *Dio*, he was ready for bed.

It was all rubbish. Rubbish, rubbish, rubbish... He should employ someone to take care of his personal life as he did his business life. Then he wouldn't have to deal with bills and the other necessary parts of life. Considering he'd abandoned running a household within weeks of having one, that thought would be funny if he hadn't lost his funny bone. Or would it be ironic? Anna had been a great one for finding irony funny. She'd found a lot of things funny. His life was a much less cheerful place without her. He hadn't noticed that when she'd left him the first time as he'd been too busy wallowing in his own sense of... What had she called it? Self-righteousness? She'd been describing herself when she'd said it but it applied to him too.

It had only been since his return from San Francisco when he'd refused himself the luxury of self-righteousness that he'd really noticed how the colour had gone from his life. Maybe it had been because she'd come back to him for that one week and they'd learned more about each other then than they had in the whole of the two and a half years they'd known each other.

Why couldn't he stop thinking of her?

He took a healthy slug of his bourbon and opened the last item of mail, a thick padded envelope with a San Francisco postmark.

This must be the gift the concierge in his apartment there had messaged him about. It had been delivered shortly after he'd left for London on the day that was his and Anna's first wedding anniversary. Not caring what was in it—not caring about anything—Stefano had told the man to forward it to his London address.

And now it was here.

Inside the packaging was a small square gift-wrapped box.

He twisted it in his hands, his heart racing as his mind drifted back to Anna's insistence on some solo 'retail therapy' that afternoon before the awards ceremony.

He'd thought it strange when she'd returned empty-handed.

He could not credit how much he missed her. It hadn't been this bad before.

No, it *had* been this bad before but he'd masked it from himself. And it had been more than self-righteousness that had masked it but a mad fury like nothing he'd ever known...

She'd made assumptions about Christina, but hadn't he made assumptions about Anna being a gold-digger? Hadn't he been as determined to see the worst in her as Anna had been to see the worst in him?

He sat bolt upright, his brain racing almost as madly as his heart.

Dio, he could see the truth.

Somewhere along the line he had fallen in love with her. The man who had spent his life avoiding serious relationships for terror of being hurt and rejected had fallen in love.

Because he *had* been terrified. For all his disdain at people who refused to let go of their childhood he could see he'd done the opposite and buried his under a 'don't care' bravado when all the time he'd been running, try-ing to stop it ever happening again.

He bent his head forward and dug his fingers into the back of his head as he strove to suck in air.

How could he have been so blind and stupid?

He'd blown it.

He loved his wife but the joke was on him because she didn't love him any more.

Breathing deeply, he looked again at the gift-wrapped box.

Feeling as if he were opening something that could bite him, he ripped the wrapping off and snapped the lid of the black square box open.

Nestled inside it were two gold wedding bands.

CHAPTER TWELVE

ANNA ACCEPTED THE bottle of water from Melissa with a grateful smile of thanks.

The sand on Bondi beach was fine and deliciously warm between her toes, the sun blazing down and baking her skin. As it was a work day and the schools were open, the beach was busy but not packed. While there wasn't the privacy she'd found at hers and Stefano's Santa Cruz beach house, there was an easy vibe that almost, *almost* gave her the peace she so longed for.

The rate she was going she would never find peace. Not in herself.

Melissa stretched out on the sun-lounger beside her and they sat there amiably, sunglasses on, soaking up the rays.

'What do you want to do later?' Melissa said after a while.

'I haven't got anything in mind. You?'

'Shall we borrow Mick's Jeep and go for a drive and explore the suburbs?'

'You'll have to drive. I haven't been behind a wheel in years.'

'All the more reason you should drive. Use it or lose it.'

Anna laughed but it was a muted sound compared to the way she used to laugh.

'Shall we invite Mum with us?' Melissa asked carefully.

'If you want.'

When Anna had flown out to Australia it hadn't been to make her peace with her mother but to make her peace with Melissa. She had been determined to do what Stefano had suggested though, and sit down and talk to her mother, if only just so she could move on.

Her mum hadn't quite seen it like that. Anna had arrived at the house to find the whole ground floor covered in balloons and banners to welcome her. All the neighbours and Mick's family had been invited round to meet her. Melissa had stood there, eyes pleading for Anna to go along with it—Anna could almost read her mind, realising her sister was begging her not to make a scene.

Making a scene was the last thing she'd wanted to do.

She'd looked at her mum, flanked by her husband and stepkids, and seen the desperate excitement in her eyes, and the fear.

Too much water had passed under the bridge for Anna to throw herself into her mother's arms as if nothing had happened but she'd returned her embrace coolly.

It had been almost a decade since she'd last seen her and she'd taken in the marked changes time had wrought. Her mother had done the same in return. They'd stared at each other for so long that Anna's eyes had blurred, her heart so full that it pushed up into her throat and then she really had fallen into her mother's arms.

As the evening had progressed and she couldn't make a move without tripping over her mother, Anna had come to understand exactly what it meant for her mum to have her youngest child under her roof and had cancelled her hotel reservation and agreed to stay there, sharing the guest room with Melissa.

That had been two weeks ago.

They had spent a long time talking. They'd been honest with each other. Many tears had been shed. A bucketful of them.

Her mother had apologised over and over for leaving her behind and for the cruel words she'd spoken the last time they'd been together. She hadn't made any excuses. She knew she'd been selfish and had effectively abandoned her daughters for the sake of a man. Her bone-deep guilt had been her punishment.

If Anna were being cynical she could say that if the guilt had been that bad, she could always have come home to them.

She didn't want to be cynical any more.

Things were still awkward at times but slowly they were forging a rapport. Perhaps they would never regain their old mother-daughter relationship but Anna was confident that when she returned to London they would retain some semblance of one. It was entirely in her hands. Whatever wrongs her mother had done, Stefano had been correct in his assessment that she had missed her. She needed her mother in her life.

She hadn't known how badly she'd needed her until she'd found her again and found the courage to let go of her anger and forgive.

She just wished the pain in her heart would ease. Not even the peace she'd made with her sister and the forgiveness she'd found for her mother had eased it. And it was getting worse, especially since Melissa had given her the pin code for her phone—it turned out she'd used Stefano's birthday—and she'd gone through all her photos and videos. There was one video where she'd sneakily filmed Stefano taking a shower. The footage showed his start of surprise when he'd spotted her, then his wolfish grin as he'd opened the glass shower door. The footage went dark when he grabbed her phone and threw it onto the floor.

He'd then grabbed *her*, she remembered, and dragged her fully clothed into the shower with him. Her clothes hadn't stayed on for much longer.

Her heart ached to think of him and when she closed her eyes all she could see was the despair on his face when she'd walked away.

She had never seen him like that before, not her strong, powerful husband. She'd seen him in passion and in anger but never in wretched defeat.

A fresh wave of pain hit her as she imagined him now and all he was having to cope with.

He'd been coping with it ever since she'd burst into his boardroom.

He was dealing with a father who'd been alive his whole life while he'd thought him dead. A father who *had* wanted him when no one else in his family had cared enough to even buy him shoes that fitted. He was dealing with a sister he hadn't known existed until a few months ago, his first true familial relationship since he'd been seven.

And now he was having to deal with the knowledge that he and Anna had conceived a child together but that its tiny life had died before he could even celebrate its conception.

She knew too that he carried guilt over his treatment of her.

It was a heavy burden for him to carry and he was having to carry it on his own.

But he probably wasn't alone, she scolded herself. This was Stefano she was thinking of; his bed was never empty for more than a week.

Immediately she castigated herself. He'd been faithful to her throughout their marriage and it was wrong of her to make assumptions now. She'd leapt to conclusions when she'd found Christina in their apartment and had been paying the price for it ever since. For all the horrendous wrongs he'd done, the only solid image in her mind was Stefano watching her leave his apartment, as haunted and haggard as she had ever seen him.

He'd asked her if they could start again...

But she'd dismissed him.

He hadn't wanted her to go.

She shook her head to clear it. She would have to see him in person soon. She needed to be strong, not let doubts creep in.

He'd had doubts. He'd tried to stop the revenge he'd plotted down to the smallest detail from being carried out.

He'd asked her if they could start again...

Discovering the truth that night in San Francisco had been the most soul-destroying thing she had ever lived through. Learning that he'd seduced her and made her fall in love with him for revenge... She'd understood all this at the same moment the awful memories of their parting and the miscarriage had come back to her. The two had become a singular issue in her mind and the pain it all had unleashed had been too much to bear.

Time apart had given her some perspective.

He'd told her he wanted to start their marriage afresh

and she'd dismissed it without properly listening to what he was saying. He'd told her he wanted to start their marriage again *after* she'd told him she loved him. This from the man who didn't do forgiveness or love.

Melissa's voice cut through her rambling thoughts. 'You okay, chook?'

'Sorry? *Chook?*'

'Mum says it's an Aussie term of endearment.'

Anna's lips twitched but that was the nearest thing to a smile she could muster.

'Anna? You okay?'

She blinked herself back into focus and shook her head. 'I don't think I am.'

'What? You're not okay?' Alarm spread across Melissa's face. 'Are you feeling unwell? Are you going to be sick again?'

'No, nothing like that. No. Mel...I think...'

'What?'

Her mind running this way and that, Anna got to her feet and started throwing her stuff into her beach bag. 'I need to go back.'

Melissa hastily slid off her sun-lounger. 'I'll come with you.'

In less than a minute they'd gathered all their stuff together and thrown their shorts and T-shirts back on and Anna was steaming along the beach, unwittingly spraying sand in sunbathers' faces, while Melissa struggled to keep up.

'Slow down,' she pleaded. 'The house isn't going anywhere.'

This time Anna did find a proper smile. 'I'm not going back to the house, I'm going to the airport.'

'What?'

'I'm going home.'

'You can't.'

'Watch me.'

'No, you idiot, I mean you can't go to the airport—your passport's at Mum's.'

'Oh. Yes. Right.' But it only slowed her for a moment and then she walked even faster, mentally calculating how quickly she could get to the airport. Her return flight was booked for a week from now. She was sure the airline had fixed flights so that would mean a plane would be leaving for London that evening. She needed to be on it.

'What do you want to go home for?'

'I need to see Stefano.'

'Anna, *no*…'

'Yes.'

'You were going to wait. Let things settle a bit more before telling him.'

'It's nothing to do with that.'

Melissa grabbed her arm and forced her to stop. 'Anna, will you listen to me? Please? Whatever you're thinking, don't do it.'

'Mel…I love him.' Totally. Utterly. Irreversibly.

'That man *destroyed* you.'

'No,' she contradicted. 'I think we've destroyed each other. And maybe we can fix each other.'

It was a fifteen-minute fast walk back to the house. Melissa was puffing behind her as Anna rushed through the front door, her adrenaline levels too high to need to catch a breath.

She hurried up the hallway to the stairs, about to go to her room and get her flight details so she could get straight on the phone to the airline…

'Anna, is that you?' came her mother's voice.

'Yes, sorry, give me a minute.'

Her mother appeared at the kitchen doorway, her face flushed. 'You've got a visitor.'

'Me?' Who would be visiting *her*? She didn't know anyone here apart from her mum's friends and family.

She stepped into the kitchen, turned her head to the large table and froze.

After several long, long moments she closed her eyes then slowly opened them again.

Stefano was sitting at the kitchen table. Her mum's golden retriever, George, had his head on his lap.

'What are you doing here?' she whispered, placing a hand to her chest to stop her heart from jumping out of it.

'Visiting you.' Slowly he rose to his feet.

She inched closer and drank in the face she hadn't seen in what felt like for ever until she was only a foot away.

A mere two weeks apart had left marked changes in him. He was paler than she remembered. His hair needed cutting. He looked as if he'd slept in his canvas shorts and crumpled shirt.

As if he could read her mind, one side of his mouth curved up and he said, 'It was a long flight.'

She couldn't think clearly. The joy bursting into life inside her was marred with caution.

He'd flown across the world to see her just as she'd been gearing up to fly across the world to see him and to find out if there was any chance of a future together for them.

But what if he was here for a different reason? What if he only wanted to discuss their divorce?

Every morning since she'd left San Francisco she'd promised herself that today would be the day she would call her lawyer in England and start proper divorce proceedings. After all, they'd been married for a full year. There was nothing to stop them.

And yet, for all her anger and misery, she hadn't been able to bring herself to do it.

Had the time apart that had been so painful to her only been a healer for him?

Until he told her his reasons for being there she would not allow the screaming excitement running through her to take control.

'Is there somewhere private we can talk?' he asked, breaking the silence that had formed while she stood there trying to catch a coherent thought.

Her mum and sister quickly shuffled out of sight but Anna didn't trust that they wouldn't listen in to what was going on.

'The garden?'

He nodded and, on legs that had gone from having bones supporting them to what felt like overcooked noodles, she led him outside. George slipped out with them before she could close the door.

Her mum's garden was a lovingly tended spot with a good-sized swimming pool. They sat carefully on the large swing chair with a canopy to shade them from the blazing sun, both making sure not to sit too close to the other. They were still close enough that Anna's body vibrated at his nearness and she had to fold her hands tightly together to stop them stretching out to touch him and feel for herself that she wasn't dreaming this.

George sat himself at Stefano's feet and he leaned down to rub the dog's head.

'I think you've made a friend,' Anna commented softly.

'I like dogs.'

She hadn't known that. 'You should get one.'

'One day. He's your mother's?'

'Yes.'

'How are things with her?'

'Better than I thought they'd be.'

'You've forgiven her?'

'Just about.' She would never be less than honest with him. 'It's so hard to let the past go but I have to. If I've learnt anything in recent months it's that holding onto anger destroys you as much as the other. She's made mistakes—massive ones—but I have too and I know she's genuinely sorry. I am too. I just want her back in my life.'

They lapsed into silence that stretched so unbearably tight that Anna couldn't endure it a moment longer. 'Why are you here?'

'Because I'm falling apart without you.' His shoulders rose and he turned his head to look at her. 'I want you to think about coming back. Not to me, I know you won't do that, but back to Moretti's. The staff are on the verge of mutiny because without you there I have lost my conscience. You can have your own office so you don't have to see me if you don't want to. You can boss me around just as well by email as in person. Name your terms and your price.'

Stefano didn't take his gaze off her. He sought every tiny flicker of reaction on her face.

Her forehead furrowed. 'You want me to come back to *work*?'

'I know I'm asking a lot of you.'

'You're not wrong.'

'Please. Hear me out. Anna, it's not just Moretti's that's falling apart, is me. *I'm* falling apart. I know you won't come back as my wife but I miss having you in my life. You keep me sane. You help me see things clearly. I need you.'

He'd never said that before to anyone. He'd learned at too young an age that people were too often faithless and cruel to each other to allow himself to ever need someone. The only person he'd ever needed was himself.

Much of the colour had left her face.

'If you come back then it will be on whatever terms you choose. Having you close by will be enough for me.' He ran his fingers through his hair to stop them from touching her. 'I know it's over for us. How I took advantage of your amnesia was unforgivable. I was furious about your assumptions that I was having an affair but I made assumptions of my own. I swore you had to be a gold-digger because I couldn't face the truth that you were in love with me and I was in love with you.'

She sucked in a breath and he grimaced. 'I know it's too late for you to hear that but, please, allow me to explain. I know I won't have your forgiveness but I would like your understanding.

'Your instincts about your promotion were right—I did give it to you so I could be rid of you—you *were* the best person for the job but that was secondary—but it wasn't because I was bored with you. You were scared I would leave you but I was already scared you would leave me. I've never been wanted for myself before, not since Nonno died. The rest of my family didn't want me and you know as well as I do that they treated me like dirt. When I left them to fend for myself, people didn't want *me*, they wanted to use me; bosses exploiting my age to try and underpay me, drunk women seeing me as nothing but a handsome face to have sex with. When I finally made my fortune people didn't want me for myself, they wanted my fame and money. You were the first person to see through the expensive suits and see the man inside. How could you like that man when no one else had ever liked or wanted him? I deliberately pushed you away because I was too much of a coward to acknowledge that I loved you. I pushed you away before you could push me.'

His soul laid bare, Stefano took a long breath and covered her hands. A glimmer of hope fluttered in him when she didn't resist, her eyes still on his face, wide and glistening.

'I can't be without you,' he said, willing for her to believe him. 'I can't even breathe normally. Days without you are an eternity. Please come back. If all you can offer is to take your place in Moretti's again then that's enough.'

Time itself seemed to morph into eternity while he waited for her to respond.

When she moved her hands out of his hold his heart sank so sharply it caused physical pain.

But then she placed one on his cheek and moved her face a little closer and his heart dared to rise back up.

'After all you've just said are you only offering me my job back?'

He trapped the hand palmed against his cheek. 'Anna, you have my heart. Whatever you can give I will accept. I need you and I will take whatever you can give.'

'But what do you *want*?'

Something in her expression sent warmth into blood that had been cold for weeks. 'I want you to ask me to make that promise I made to you again so that I can tell you I don't need to make it because there will never be anyone else but you for me.'

Slowly her face moved to his and then her eyes closed and her lips pressed gently against his.

He hardly dared to breathe. He'd flown out here knowing he needed to make that one last move and strip himself bare for her. He'd reconciled himself to them being over but had been unable to reconcile with Anna being out of his life for good. She was so much a part of him that her not being there had been like living with a piece of himself missing.

'I don't want to come back to London as your employee,' she whispered into his mouth. 'I want to come back as your wife.'

This was more than he had dared hope for. Far more. 'You do?'

Her nose brushed his as she nodded. 'I love you.'

A boulder settled in his throat and he swallowed it away. 'But can you forgive me?'

'We've both made mistakes. If we can't draw a line under them and make a fresh start then we'll both suffer for it.' She smiled, though her chin wobbled. 'It's been agony for me without you. I'd already decided to come home and see if there was any chance for us.'

'Really?'

She nodded. 'That's why I came back early from the beach. It had all suddenly become clear for me. I thought my love for you had died but that was my hurt and pride talking, not my heart.'

'I swear I will never do anything to hurt you again.'

'We're both stubborn and fiery. We'll probably spend the rest of our lives arguing with each other.'

'As long as we spend the rest of it making up then I can live with that.' And to prove his point he put a hand round the back of her head and pulled her in for another kiss, this one deep and full of all the love and desire he felt for this beautiful woman without whom he was nothing but a shell of himself.

She was everything to him, his lover, his confidante and his sparring partner. It would be easier to live without a limb than without her.

'How do you feel about us becoming parents?' she asked him between kisses.

He put his finger under her chin.

For all that they'd forgiven each other everything, Anna being alone when she miscarried their child was something he would never forgive himself for.

'When the time is right we can try for a child. I want us to have a football team of *bambinos* and a couple of dogs for them to play with but not until you're ready for it.'

He thought he would see sadness in her eyes but they were bright and...knowing.

'Anna?'

Suddenly the most enormous grin beamed from her face.

'You're not?'

'I am.' She snuggled into him, her head on his chest. 'I took the test last week.'

'With Melissa?' he asked drily. This was unbelievable. He'd left London feeling as if he were drowning, seeking Anna as a life raft, and now felt as if the sun were shining especially for them.

'Yes.'

'And one for luck?'

'Yes.' She pressed herself even tighter to him. 'Neither of us knew it at the time but I wasn't protected when we were in Santa Cruz—I never had another injection after

I lost...' The kiss on her head and the tightening of the arms around her showed that Stefano understood what she was struggling to vocalise. 'I'm sorry for not telling you sooner,' she whispered into his chest. 'I was trying to get my head around it and I knew it was something I had to tell you to your face. But I was going to tell you as soon as I got back to London. I swear.'

He ran his fingers through her hair. 'Don't apologise. I know you would have told me. How are you feeling?'

'A little sick at times but nothing to complain about.' Her face shone as she gazed up at him. 'And you?'

He kissed her. 'I feel that you've given me all my birthday and Christmas presents in one go.'

And speaking of presents...

He disentangled himself just enough to pull out the small black square box he'd carried on his person since he'd opened it a week ago.

She recognised it at once, her eyes widening and somehow brightening further. 'I was going to give you that...'

'On our wedding anniversary,' he finished for her.

She held out her left hand for him and he slid the smaller ring onto her wedding finger then kissed it. 'I love you.'

'I love you too,' she whispered before taking the larger ring and sliding it onto his finger and kissing it in turn.

It took a long time for Stefano to comprehend the magnitude of all that had happened, how his last throw of the dice had brought him rewards he'd not allowed himself to dream of.

He had his wife back and this time he would honour and cherish her until his dying breath.

EPILOGUE

ANNA SAT ON the side of the bath watching Stefano, who was leaning against the wall looking at his watch, light bouncing off his gold wedding band, a white oblong stick in his hand.

The bathroom door was shoved open and Cecily, their three-year-old daughter, came flying in followed in quick succession by her four-year-old brother and their slower, sappy King Charles spaniel, Alfie.

Cecily threw her arms around Anna's legs. 'Mario hit me,' she wailed.

'She threw my ice cream on the floor!' he hollered indignantly.

'Behave, the pair of you,' Stefano scolded, amusement lurking in his eyes. 'And no hitting.'

'But…!'

'If you can't play nicely together we won't go to the beach,' Anna cut in. With Mario due to start school in England that September, they'd decided to spend the summer in their Santa Cruz beach house, the unanimous family favourite of all their homes.

Two months before Mario had been born, they'd left their London apartment and moved into a rambling manor house in Oxfordshire surrounded by acres of land for their football team of children to play in. It was an idyllic existence. Picture perfect. Apart from having two children who liked nothing more than fighting furiously, of course.

'No fair!' they both shouted together. Still bickering, the pair of them toddled off to their playroom, no doubt leaving a trail of chaos and destruction in their wake. She found it remarkable that their mess didn't bother her at all.

'Are you sure you want another one?' Stefano asked, laughing.

She grinned. Their football team hadn't quite materialised. After having two children with a gap of less than a year between them, they'd decided to wait and enjoy them before having any more.

She'd come off the pill a month ago.

'I think we can cope.'

'That's a relief.' He passed the stick to her, his grin now as wide as his face. 'Because according to this, we're having another one.'

Anna read the blue plus sign, her own grin widening to match her husband's.

With a whoop of delight, Stefano picked her up and planted kisses all over her face.

Wrapping her legs around his waist and her arms around his neck, Anna returned the kisses. Even with two children and another on the way, their desire and love for each other remained undiminished. There wasn't a single aspect of her life she would change. Together they'd created a family filled with love and laughter, arguments and *lots* of making up.

'Daddy! What are you doing to my mummy?' Cecily was standing in the bathroom doorway, her arms folded and the same expression on her face that Stefano always used when he wasn't amused by something. 'Put her down at once!'

Stefano put Anna down, gave her one last kiss for luck, then scooped his daughter up and carried her, screaming with laughter, upside down to the playroom.

* * * * *

If you enjoyed ONCE A MORETTI WIFE,
why not explore these other
Michelle Smart stories?

MARRIED FOR THE GREEK'S CONVENIENCE
CLAIMING HIS CHRISTMAS CONSEQUENCE
WEDDED, BEDDED, BETRAYED
TALOS CLAIMS HIS VIRGIN
THESEUS DISCOVERS HIS HEIR

Available now!

MILLS & BOON®
Hardback – April 2017

ROMANCE

The Italian's One-Night Baby	Lynne Graham
The Desert King's Captive Bride	Annie West
Once a Moretti Wife	Michelle Smart
The Boss's Nine-Month Negotiation	Maya Blake
The Secret Heir of Alazar	Kate Hewitt
Crowned for the Drakon Legacy	Tara Pammi
His Mistress with Two Secrets	Dani Collins
The Argentinian's Virgin Conquest	Bella Frances
Stranded with the Secret Billionaire	Marion Lennox
Reunited by a Baby Bombshell	Barbara Hannay
The Spanish Tycoon's Takeover	Michelle Douglas
Miss Prim and the Maverick Millionaire	Nina Singh
Their One Night Baby	Carol Marinelli
Forbidden to the Playboy Surgeon	Fiona Lowe
A Mother to Make a Family	Emily Forbes
The Nurse's Baby Secret	Janice Lynn
The Boss Who Stole Her Heart	Jennifer Taylor
Reunited by Their Pregnancy Surprise	Louisa Heaton
The Ten-Day Baby Takeover	Karen Booth
Expecting the Billionaire's Baby	Andrea Laurence

MILLS & BOON®
Large Print – April 2017

ROMANCE

A Di Sione for the Greek's Pleasure	Kate Hewitt
The Prince's Pregnant Mistress	Maisey Yates
The Greek's Christmas Bride	Lynne Graham
The Guardian's Virgin Ward	Caitlin Crews
A Royal Vow of Convenience	Sharon Kendrick
The Desert King's Secret Heir	Annie West
Married for the Sheikh's Duty	Tara Pammi
Winter Wedding for the Prince	Barbara Wallace
Christmas in the Boss's Castle	Scarlet Wilson
Her Festive Doorstep Baby	Kate Hardy
Holiday with the Mystery Italian	Ellie Darkins

HISTORICAL

Bound by a Scandalous Secret	Diane Gaston
The Governess's Secret Baby	Janice Preston
Married for His Convenience	Eleanor Webster
The Saxon Outlaw's Revenge	Elisabeth Hobbes
In Debt to the Enemy Lord	Nicole Locke

MEDICAL

Waking Up to Dr Gorgeous	Emily Forbes
Swept Away by the Seductive Stranger	Amy Andrews
One Kiss in Tokyo...	Scarlet Wilson
The Courage to Love Her Army Doc	Karin Baine
Reawakened by the Surgeon's Touch	Jennifer Taylor
Second Chance with Lord Branscombe	Joanna Neil

MILLS & BOON®
Hardback – May 2017

ROMANCE

The Sheikh's Bought Wife	Sharon Kendrick
The Innocent's Shameful Secret	Sara Craven
The Magnate's Tempestuous Marriage	Miranda Lee
The Forced Bride of Alazar	Kate Hewitt
Bound by the Sultan's Baby	Carol Marinelli
Blackmailed Down the Aisle	Louise Fuller
Di Marcello's Secret Son	Rachael Thomas
The Italian's Vengeful Seduction	Bella Frances
Conveniently Wed to the Greek	Kandy Shepherd
His Shy Cinderella	Kate Hardy
Falling for the Rebel Princess	Ellie Darkins
Claimed by the Wealthy Magnate	Nina Milne
Mummy, Nurse...Duchess?	Kate Hardy
Falling for the Foster Mum	Karin Baine
The Doctor and the Princess	Scarlet Wilson
Miracle for the Neurosurgeon	Lynne Marshall
English Rose for the Sicilian Doc	Annie Claydon
Engaged to the Doctor Sheikh	Meredith Webber
The Marriage Contract	Kat Cantrell
Triplets for the Texan	Janice Maynard

MILLS & BOON®
Large Print – May 2017

ROMANCE

A Deal for the Di Sione Ring	Jennifer Hayward
The Italian's Pregnant Virgin	Maisey Yates
A Dangerous Taste of Passion	Anne Mather
Bought to Carry His Heir	Jane Porter
Married for the Greek's Convenience	Michelle Smart
Bound by His Desert Diamond	Andie Brock
A Child Claimed by Gold	Rachael Thomas
Her New Year Baby Secret	Jessica Gilmore
Slow Dance with the Best Man	Sophie Pembroke
The Prince's Convenient Proposal	Barbara Hannay
The Tycoon's Reluctant Cinderella	Therese Beharrie

HISTORICAL

The Wedding Game	Christine Merrill
Secrets of the Marriage Bed	Ann Lethbridge
Compromising the Duke's Daughter	Mary Brendan
In Bed with the Viking Warrior	Harper St. George
Married to Her Enemy	Jenni Fletcher

MEDICAL

The Nurse's Christmas Gift	Tina Beckett
The Midwife's Pregnancy Miracle	Kate Hardy
Their First Family Christmas	Alison Roberts
The Nightshift Before Christmas	Annie O'Neil
It Started at Christmas...	Janice Lynn
Unwrapped by the Duke	Amy Ruttan

417 GEN STD LP

MILLS & BOON®

Why shop at millsandboon.co.uk?

Each year, thousands of romance readers find their perfect read at millsandboon.co.uk. That's because we're passionate about bringing you the very best romantic fiction. Here are some of the advantages of shopping at www.millsandboon.co.uk:

* **Get new books first**—you'll be able to buy your favourite books one month before they hit the shops

* **Get exclusive discounts**—you'll also be able to buy our specially created monthly collections, with up to 50% off the RRP

* **Find your favourite authors**—latest news, interviews and new releases for all your favourite authors and series on our website, plus ideas for what to try next

* **Join in**—once you've bought your favourite books, don't forget to register with us to rate, review and join in the discussions

Visit **www.millsandboon.co.uk**
for all this and more today!